The Mystic Muse

The Mystic Muse

J.J. Tharakan

PARTRIDGE

A Penguin Random House Company

To order additional copies of this book, contact
Partridge India
000 800 10062 62
orders.india@partridgepublishing.com

www.partridgepublishing.com/india

Contents

Prologue

Storms are awesome but tsunamis are surely the mother of all storms. This is the story of one such giant wave which played the role of the hand of fate in the lives of a few special people. It altered their lives beyond their wildest dreams but if you asked anyone of them the reason for the drastic changes in their lives, they would have difficulty in remembering the tsunami as the cause of it all. But it was. A secret agent. An agent of subterfuge.

And this was how the tsunami was born.

Under the glittering surface of the deep blue sea, miles below the surface and deep in the crust of the earth, there was a super slow stirring. Giant tectonic plates shifted in nanometers, a slight movement in the massive, impenetrable structure of the earth. From the epicenter of the earth quake, waves of disturbance spread through the earth's plates and rippled across the ocean bed.

The great ocean curled in on itself, its shoreline receding far below the water line of the lowest astronomical tide. In the sky the stars and sun shone their light, impassive, unchanging, down on the earth and the cosmos spun in its eternal, timeless motion while the tsunami prepared to flood the shore. Once again, in a small corner of the planet, a small few people would experience the devastating and life changing power of nature.

On that fateful day, the rising sun was still a murky red, late in the morning. This was a warning in the sky for those who could read the portents of nature. But, in today's world of instantaneous communication, who on earth has the time (or the inclination) in their busy, busy lives to look up, look around, breathe in deeply and see and feel the elements of nature, or even disaster, staring them right in the face? There are people paid to do just that. But sometimes, even the watchers don't see enough. The warnings, when they came, would be too late. Too little. And futile.

The ocean gathered in on itself, preparing to fling its waters far inland and lay imperious claim to the land. No one was aware. No one paid it any heed. Deep into the sea, the waters recoiled and receded and then, slowly at first and then building up into an unstoppable, elemental momentum, a giant wave commenced its inexorable passage to the shore. The tsunami was born and before it died, it would claim more than a few lives cause much destruction and change forever the course of several lives. And now heed my story.

****

Chapter One

Karan Kasper sat at the piano and gazed at the bare wall against which the instrument stood. He had his notebook open, ready to jot down whenever inspiration struck him. Unfortunately, his mind was as blank as the wall he was staring at. He ran his fingers across the keys and hit a low note. He felt despondent, terrible. There was no worse feeling for a creative artist then when his creation is stillborn. He mused for a while and then played a lower note. Nothing. Now he felt even worse. Misery in a minor chord. At this rate he was never going to get the jingle down. He played a few more notes and then got up from the piano and walked across the room to the window of his apartment.

Karan gazed down at the traffic on the road. It was a busy morning as usual and he could hear the endless drone of the morning traffic interspersed with the shrill beeping of horns. The symphony of the road, he thought. He was getting better at naming music then writing it. He moved impatiently away from the window. What he needed was a nice long walk. Maybe inspiration would strike him while he was mobile.

Karan decided he would walk to the beach which was not very far from his apartment. The sea breeze would refresh him and he could try and sort out his thoughts. He left the flat and began to run down the stairs, avoiding the lift which was slow and invariably busy.

As he trotted down the stairs from the 4th floor, he came across his neighbor, Mistry, puffing and panting his way up the stairs. Mistry was a youngish man about Karan's own age, which is to say about thirty. They were good and close friends of a sort, but their companionship was somewhat constrained because of the fact that Mistry was married while Karan was not. Mistry's wife regarded Karan with deep suspicion, convinced he was a waster, alcoholic and sex fiend as well. Mistry was more pleasant natured and glad of Karan's company when he could get away from his wife. Karan's single life reminded Mistry of his own bachelor days and he envied his friend his freedom and despised him for his loneliness at the same time.

"Hey, Mistry!" Karan greeted his friend. "Has the elevator broken down?"

"No," replied his friend. "My treadmill has broken down and this the only way I am going to get any exercise. Where are you off to? I thought you had an important jingle to write."

"Yeah, but it isn't working out so I'm going to try and clear my head and then start again. By the way, there's a girl coming to my flat later in the morning. She is a singer and voice over artist and she's coming to help me do the basic recording for my tune. So don't get any wrong notions about what this girl is doing in my flat."

"Are you worried about your reputation?" asked Mistry, leaning a hand against the wall and gasping for breath. His large stomach moved rhythmically in time to his breathing, "you don't need to worry because it can't get any worse."

His breathing steadied a bit and he perked up. "I say, is she pretty?"

"Why would you want to know?" asked Karan "anyway, I haven't seen her yet."

"I'll bet she is," said Mistry wistfully starting his climb again. "You lucky dog"

Karan continued his descent

"Well, if she hits a high note it'll only be because we are recording," he said, disappearing out of sight down the stairwell.

"I'll believe that," said Mistry sarcastically. He glanced up the stairwell, calculating how much further he had to climb. He was a stock trader by profession and he spent his life estimating risk and benefit. Shaking his head in dismay at the number of steps left to climb, he resumed his weary trudge up the stairs.

Chapter Two

Karan left the building feeling better already. The run down the stairs had instantly revived his good humor. He crossed the road and bought a bottle of lemonade from a roadside vendor. Soon he was at the beach and he opened the cap on the bottle and washed his throat down with the tangy drink.

Glancing over the water and at the clear blue sky, he took a few deep breaths to clear his chest and then begin to sing,

"Do ray, do ray".

He sang the scales a few times, starting at the top and lingering over each note. An old couple out for their morning constitutional heard him caterwauling and moved warily away, looking at him curiously as they continued their stroll on the beach. Karan ignored them as well as the other onlookers and strollers. He felt fine.

He started again, closing his eyes "Do-ray, Do-ray" and then he went up the scale "Do-ray-me-fa-so-la-ti do!" He did this several times. By the time he had finished, a couple of hawkers, two weight lifters with intimidating physiques, one old woman dressed in shorts and a couple of stray dogs, their tails quivering, had gathered around him. He stopped and opened his eyes and they gave him a round of applause.

Even the dogs barked enthusiastically. Karan bowed to his audience and set off along the beach. He repeated the scales mentally over and over again, imagining the pitch and tone. Gradually he began to get the idea for his jingle.

The subject matter of the commercial was a washing machine. That did not matter in the composition; it just had to be catchy and upbeat. And unique. Ideally, everyone who heard it would be humming it all the way to the appliance store and singing it out loud as they brought the washing machine home. This was an important assignment for Karan because if he could make this work he would get a lot more jobs from the ad agency. He had begged and pleaded with them for a break and they had tossed him this bone. Now all he had to do was deliver on his promise.

He hummed the scales over and over, at the same time reviewing and rejecting several tunes that popped up in his head.

The air was crisp and sharp. A fresh breeze blowing from the vast ocean caressed his hair. Karan looked across the water at the horizon. The sky had a reddish tinge, unusual at this time of the day. The water had receded more than it normally did. He could see various objects the tide had left behind on the sand, seashells and starfish. A crowd of people had walked to the edge of the retreating water, exclaiming and remarking about the strange color of the sky. Karan walked on, repeating the scales in his head like a mantra.

His lemonade was finished and he detoured off the beach to get another bottle. A young woman dressed in a summer skirt and carrying a bottle of cola smiled at him. Nice, thought Karan. If he wasn't busy, he might have accepted what seemed like an invitation but not today. He had to complete composing the tune today. The vendor gave him another lemonade and asked if Karan was going for a swim. Not this time, he replied and set off again along the beach sipping his drink.

He walked for another twenty minutes before a seemingly promising sounding tune firmed up in his mind. It seemed to have potential. Karan stopped walking and turned to gaze at the sea again. He tried to bring the tune up to the surface of his mind, humming a little. Now he felt more confident. It was a six bar tune, which would be the main refrain for his jingle. He played around with it, adding a note and dropping another. He had it now. He clenched his fist in the air and began to sing out loud. This time there was no one around to applaud. After voicing the tune several times, he pulled out his diary and made a notation.

That was it. All he had to do now was find words to rhyme with washing machine and then he was done. He hoped the girl from the talent agency was good. He could get this thing done today and do the final recording tomorrow. With a little luck by the end of the week he would get paid and then he would have the money to pay the rent on his apartment. Checking the time on his watch he realized he should be heading back to his apartment now. The girl would be coming soon. He turned to go and noticed the reddish hue on the horizon again. Almost everyone else on the beach was staring at the sky and the distant waterline. The ocean had receded even further and now it must have been at least several hundred meters more than usual. Very strange, he thought absently. He wondered if there was a storm coming. Little did he know.

Leaving the beach he crossed the road and headed towards his apartment. People were thronging to the beach to see the strange phenomenon they had heard about on the streets and he had to fight his way through the crowd. He thought he must be the only one moving away from the water. Keeping his head down, he doggedly fought his way through the crowd. In his mind he played his new tune over and over. Finally he was clear of the throng and the apartment was now only a short distance away.

Karan decided to speed up his heart rate to get another endorphin rush like he had when he raced down the stairs on the way to the beach. He broke into a run. Entering the apartment, he sped up the steps, his hand gliding over the hand rail. He ran up four flights of stairs and arrived at his flat panting in exhaustion. He stopped for a while at the top of the stairs, breathing in great heaving gasps and holding his sides. After he had rested a while, he moved towards his flat, on the other side of the stairwell.

As he approached his apartment he saw a very pretty girl, smartly dressed, standing at his door. She was reaching her hand out to ring his door bell. Karan still struggling to catch his breath, admiring the girl who had not yet noticed him. He wondered if the agency had made a mistake and sent him a model instead of a singer. As he moved closer to the door, she turned and looked at him in sudden alarm. He was still breathing heavily and couldn't find his voice. Trying to get his breath under control, he held up a hand to reassure her but, still startled, she moved a few steps away from him to be safe. Karan studied her while he caught his breath.

The girl's hair was cut in an aggressive page boy style, with sharp waves angling across her forehead. Her face was slightly angular with protruding cheekbones and otherwise regular features. She wore bright lipstick but no other make -up. Interesting, thought Karan, very interesting.

Now it was her turn to put her hand out in the air, as if to stop him from coming any closer.

"Have you come to see Mr. Kaspar? I think he is not in," she said. She had a clear, high musical voice, Karan noticed.

He ran a hand through his windblown hair and straightened his shoulders.

"I am he," he said, realizing too late how pompous he sounded.

"Who?" asked the girl, backing away a little more till she was close to the far wall.

Karan's shoulders slumped. "Let's start again," he said.

"I'm Karan Kaspar," he said, his voice a little more firm. "And you must be the girl from VSpot, the talent agency"

Now it was the girl's turn to straighten up. She ran a hand through her immaculate hair and then held it out.

"Pleased to meet you, Mr. Karan," she said. Karan took the proffered hand and marveled at how soft and warm it was. He held on to it a little longer than necessary and she yanked it back quickly.

"My name is Stella. Yes, I am the play back artist from VSpot," said the girl.

"Yes, well, good," said Karan, flustered again. His hand still held the imprint of the girl's delicate fingers. He fished in his pocket for his keys, pulled them out, dropped them and bent over to pick them up. Stella backed up even more till she was against the wall.

"Just let me get this door open and then we can get in and get started," said Karan, fumbling with the lock. Finally he had the door open and he motioned her to step in. The girl took a cautious peek into the flat and then walked slowly in. Karan came in behind her and then turned and closed the door. The thud of the door slamming shut caused the girl to jump.

"Relax, Stella," said Karan, more confident now that he was in the house. He placed his keys on a shelf and walked into the living room. Stella laughed self consciously. "I guess I am a little nervous," she said. "I've never done this before."

Now it was Karan's turn to be suspicious. "Never done what before?" he asked.

"I've never actually sung before," she said. Seeing the expression in his face she added quickly, "I've done plenty of voice over but never actually recorded my singing."

"Oh," said Karan. That's why he had got her at the discount rates, thought Karan. Still she had a sweet voice so she should be okay.

"Well, the procedure is a bit primitive, I'm afraid. We'll work out the tune and the jingle now. I've got some recording equipment, nothing fancy, but it will do for now. After we get in some practice, tomorrow we go into the studio and do the cut."

"Okay," said the young girl, seeming more comfortable now. She put her bag on the sofa and sat down. Karan wondered whether he should offer her a drink. Yes, of course.

"Would you like some lemonade?" he asked, holding out the half empty bottle that he was carrying.

There were traces of sand on it from the beach and something greasy had attached itself to the side of the bottle. Stella shivered a little in disgust.

"No, thank you," she said primly. "Just some water please. For my voice," she added

Karan went to the kitchen and brought a glass of water to her. She sipped at the glass twice and set it down.

"Okay," said Karan "we might as well get started," said Karan. Better to keep this strictly professional, he thought.

He sat at the piano and picked out the tune he had composed. He repeated it a few times till it sounded about right. Then he played it again, vocalizing wordlessly as he played.

"Got it?" he asked

Stella looked at him blankly.

"Got what?" she asked

Karan sighed. "The tune," he said patiently. "Listen carefully to the tune and then see if you can sing along"

"But I don't know the words," said the girl plaintively.

"Words don't matter. It's just a jingle. We'll fill in that later. Just voice the tune and see if you can match the pitch."

"I'll play it a few times for you again."

He repeated the melody a few times. It was really quite catchy, he thought.

"Now you try it. Sing after me," he rang out the scales twice on the piano and waved his hand for her to start.

She started slowly, hesitant at first, and then with a stronger voice and totally off key. Karan quickly interrupted her. "No, no," he said. "Listen."

He sang the tune again and she tried. And she tried. And she tried again till finally Karan put his hands over his ears in frustration.

"Stop! Stop!" he cried. "You're murdering the song. Who ever told you that you could sing?"

Right in front of his eyes her face crumpled like a used paper tissue. First her lips trembled uncontrollably, her eyes became large and round like two saucers with water in them and then she was bawling, tears spurting out of her eyes like fountains.

"WAH!" she cried. Gone was all her poise and make up. She was a little girl again who had been scolded severely by her parent.

"WAH," she continued, bawling helplessly.

Karan grew frantic. He had sensitive ears and this was the worst sound he had ever heard. He had no idea what to do. He rushed to the cupboard in the dining room and pulled out a bunch of tissues. He handed them to her.

"Don't cry," he said. "Please. Don't cry. We'll try again. You can do it with practice."

It took almost fifteen minutes to quiet her down and then she had to repair her face so she spent another fifteen minutes in the bathroom.

When she came out she marched straight to the living room and picked up her handbag "I'm leaving," she told him, her voice ringing with determination and her face the picture of affronted dignity.

"Why?" asked Karan.

"Because I can't sing," she said. "I'm just a play back artist, not a singer and anyway I don't feel very well."

Karan saw another angle that he could use to cheer her up.

"What's wrong?" he asked, trying to sound solicitous.

She screwed up her face and for a minute he thought she was going to cry again.

"I don't know," she said. "My head feels funny and I keep hearing this crazy tune in my head. It always happens before I ..." she stopped suddenly.

"Before what?" Karan asked

"Never mind," said Stella. "I can't sing, really. I'm just good at voice over. They sent me here because they had no one else and I thought I might as well give it a try. Goodbye," she said, heading out the door.

"Wait, wait," said Karan, running after her. "I'll walk down with you.

Later on he was never sure why he had done this. If he had just said goodbye at the door and watched her go, his life would have remained the same. Now he was going to experience a tsunami of changes.

She waited at the elevator while he locked his apartment and they both rode down in silence. When they reached the ground floor, she said goodbye again.

"Let me buy you a coffee," said Karan. "it is the least that I can do after you have taken the trouble to come all this way" Again, in retrospect, he wondered at his actions. This would be his second and last chance to let her go,

She hesitated and then agreed. "Okay,"

Chapter Three

Karan and Stella headed down the road together. Karan led her to a coffee shop situated just off the beach. It was deserted and he was surprised at the lack of customers. Then he remembered the crowd gathering at the beach earlier this morning.

They sat down and ordered two lattes.

"Where is everybody?" asked Stella, looking around her. "Is it normally this empty?"

"No," said Karan "it is usually quite full at this time of day. I think everyone has gone to the beach."

"What's happening at the beach?" asked Stella, arranging her purse on the table and brushing back her hair with her fingers

"I don't know some strange meteorological phenomenon. I was there this morning, that's where I was coming back from when I met you at the door. I noticed that the waterline has receded considerably more than it usually does and at the horizon the sky was reddish. That's facing west in the morning so it is a very unusual color at that particular time of the day."

Stella rubbed her forehead. "I keep thinking about water. Water rising and flowing everywhere. Ever since I woke up this morning I've been thinking about it."

Karan was intrigued.

"Did you have some kind of strange dream last night?" he asked.

"I don't know," said Stella. "I never remember my dreams. But this kind of feeling is not new for me. I get this every now and then."

"Get what?" asked Karan, rubbing his own forehead and wondering if he should have just let her go. He didn't know it but it was too late for that now. Far too late.

Stella leaned forward and spoke softly, as if she were imparting a tremendous secret. "I hear this tune in my head and I have a strange sense of foreboding." she said, her voice soft and intense "and you know what? Whatever I've been thinking of comes true!"

She leaned back and regarded Karan, a curious expression on her face, a mixture of triumph and excitement and fear.

This is a nutcase, thought Karan. "What comes true?"

Stella leaned forward again and whispered, "I can see the future!!"

Karan stared at her, wondering again how quickly he could leave.

She held his gaze. "Not always, but often. I get a premonition and it comes true. You must believe me. You must!" She spoke urgently, insistent, almost pleading.

The waiter brought two iced lattes to their table. Karan wondered how long it would take her to finish her drink. He was regretting having asked her for a coffee. He should have just let her go and told the agency to send someone else.

"I haven't told anyone else about my special ability," said Stella, stirring her drink with the straw.

Karan wished she hadn't told him.

Stella sipped her latte and rubbed her temple. "I keep hearing this maddening tune in my head," she said. "It happens every time I get a premonition"

Karan looked out through the door of the cafe. On the street, traffic was whizzing by.

"So you think there are going to be floods soon?" he asked, looking up at the cloudless blue sky through the glass doors of the restaurant.

"Water everywhere," said Stella, sipping her latte again and leaning back with a look of great satisfaction, as if she had imparted a valuable secret to him.

The waiter approached their table bearing two glasses of water. As he came closer, he stumbled and the glasses toppled over on his tray splashing water onto their table and on to Stella's skirt. She shrieked and jumped up.

The waiter apologized profusely and ran to get a cloth. Stella stood, surveying her skirt which was soaked.

Karan laughed. "There's your flood," he said. Stella gave him a furious look and stalked off to the washroom to tidy herself up.

Karan watched her go, thinking that she was cute. It was a real pity that she happened to be a little crazy as well.

The waiter came with a cloth and proceeded to mop up the spilt water. Karan stood up and ambled to the door way of the cafe. He thought he could hear a commotion out on the streets. He glanced out and spotted a few people running across the road, away from the beach. Just then he felt a tremor. He put his hand out to grasp a nearby table and steady himself. What was that, he thought? He saw more people running across the street. On the far side there was a row of buildings and beyond that was the beach. More and more people were running, shouting something he could not make out. A terrorist attack, thought Karan. There was another tremor and he steadied himself again. A bomb blast?

Now the waiters and the few other people in the cafe were flocking to the entrance, watching the crowd surging away from the beach. Karan glanced to the washroom He wished Stella would come out so that they could leave. He was beginning to feel nervous.

Just then he heard someone yell, "Tsunami!". Karan glanced towards the road again and saw a huge wave of water rushing past the buildings on the other side of the street and surging across the road, towards the cafe.

In a tumult, thrashing and screaming the staff and the few other people in the cafe thronged to the door. Karan watched them go, knowing he should leave the building quickly but he was frozen to the spot. He could only think of what Stella had told him. He turned back towards the interior of the restaurant and began to move slowly towards the washroom. Just then there was an ominous rumble and the building began to shake. As if in a dream, he saw the walls of the restaurant fall inwards and parts of the ceiling begin to collapse. At the same instant almost, the door to the washroom opened and Stella stood there. She seemed frozen, a part of the furniture Then a piece of the ceiling fell between them and she screamed. He could not see her anymore. Karan turned to the exit which was a few meters away from him and still clear when he heard Stella scream again. He hesitated. Cursing her and himself he started in Stella's direction again and then more of the ceiling came down and something hit him in the shoulder and he fell on to the floor.

The terrible shaking continued for a while longer and then stopped. It was silent, except for the sound of the girl whimpering and sobbing. Karan dragged himself up, rubbing his shoulder and moved towards the sound. By the faint light which was still there, he could see her lying on the ground, arms flaying helplessly. There was a piece of masonry over her lower body. Karan was horrified. He looked into her eyes and saw the mute fear in them. He tried to drag the stone away but it was too large and heavy for him to budge. Stella screamed again, a long helpless wail, more a lament then a plea for help. Her voice echoed in the abandoned building.

Chapter Four

After a while, Stella was quiet. Karan put her hand to her face. It was cold and clammy to the touch. He looked into her eyes and saw that they were glazed, as, if a semi-transparent curtain had been drawn around them. She didn't seem to be in extreme pain, at least not consciously. Karan sat down next to her. There was no place to go. They were trapped, in the dark, under the ruins of a collapsed building.

Stella was still whimpering and moaning and Karan reached out a hand to her again. She grasped his hand with both of hers and held on to it tight.

"Don't leave me," she sobbed. "Please don't leave me."

"I won't," said Karan, looking around them. He couldn't leave if he wanted to. Directly above his head there was a large hole and he could see through to the ceiling of the floor above them. It had dangerous looking cracks running across it but was still holding. Another tremor would cause it to collapse and then it would fall directly on them. Karan whispered a prayer.

There was still electric power in the building. What little light they had was coming from a source in the floor above their heads. It seemed a possible escape avenue but they had no way of reaching up there. But help, if it came, could possibly come from that direction.

Stella was quiet now, either asleep or unconscious. Karan decided to explore the area, see if there was another way out. He slowly withdrew his hand from the girl's. She didn't stir. Karan got up and walked around. There was a little free space around them and the walls and door that led to the kitchen were intact. The other three sides were blocked with rubble. There was no way that they could pass through to the exit without some major help in shifting the stones. And that was supposing Stella could be freed from the rubble that had fallen over her lower body.

Karan pushed open the kitchen door. He walked in past the door and looked around. The far side of the room was a mass of shattered masonry, effectively blocking any chance of exit from that side. The nearer walls and the ceiling above were intact and that was what had probably saved their lives. The good news was that there was a fridge which, Karan saw when he opened it, was stacked with bottled water. Karan pulled out a couple of bottles and went back to Stella. By the feeble light which came through the collapsed ceiling, he saw that her eyes were closed. He sat down next to her and opened a bottle of water. Taking a sip he looked up at the hole in the ceiling and waited.

After a while he heard Stella stir. He turned to her and she opened her eyes. It took a few minutes for her to recollect the situation. Then she glance, horrified, at the stones covering her torso. She began to wail.

"Hush," said Karan, "we'll be out of here soon. They are coming for us."

His voice calmed her down a little.

"Are you sure?" she asked rubbing her hands across her eyes.

"Yes," said Karan, lying confidently. "They will be here very soon. Is there a lot of pain?"

Stella looked at him and her face was that of a child alone and scared in the dark.

"I can't feel my legs," she whispered.

Karan patted her shoulder.

"You'll be fine," he said. He brought the bottle of water to her lips. She raised her head to drink and he put his arm around her neck while she swallowed the water thirstily.

When she had drunk her full, he gently lowered her head till it was resting on the floor again. Karan uncurled his arm from around her neck and capped the bottle. He placed it next to him on the floor. At least they wouldn't have to worry about water, he thought. Maybe there would be some food in the fridge as well. He would check later. Not for the first time, he wished he had bought a cell phone.

"Karan," Stella spoke softly and he turned to her. "Why did you come back?"

He looked at her blankly.

"Why did you come back for me?" Stella asked again. "You could have escaped out the door very easily."

Karan didn't know what to say. "It seemed the right thing to do," he said, embarrassed.

"I'll never forget it." Stella whispered, putting her arm on his. "Whether we live or die, I'll never forget that you came back for me when you could have got away and saved your own life."

Karan looked down, avoiding her shining eyes. In truth, he didn't know why he had done what he did. Which wasn't very much, as far as he could make out.

From where he sat he could see Stella's feet. He noticed she was wearing red sandals with a bright red silk bow at the point where the straps of the sandals crossed, near her toes. Her nails were painted crimson and the effect of the silk bow juxtaposed with blood red toe nails was slightly erotic, thought Karan. He realized that his thoughts were inappropriate. She was badly injured and they were trapped in a ruined building. They could die here. He turned his eyes away from the girl's feet, so vulnerable and innocent in their beauty. He gazed into the dark interior of the building.

They sat in somber silence, awaiting their fate.

Chapter Five

Outside the building there was chaos. Water raged in the street, churning and splashing and flowing along the road. The storm surge had not subsided yet, though its intensity was less now. The earthquake had been not been too severe but several buildings had collapsed along the waterfront and across the road. The tsunami had been more devastating. Overturned and abandoned cars were lying by the side of the road. Adding to the disaster was the wide scale panic as people fled the areas along the waterfront.

When the waters began to slowly retreat, a rescue team began to approach the stricken buildings. They had trouble, the water was still high in the road and they had to wade through. Police kept gawkers and bystanders away. Most of the rescue operations were carried out by the army. It had been only three hours since the tsunami and earthquake had struck the city simultaneously. The city's response had been quick and efficient. The main areas affected were the beach front properties, most of which been flooded and some buildings had collapsed. The authorities focused their efforts on the fallen buildings, with the rescue team approaching each one and trying to determine if there was anyone trapped in the ruins. The water made their job more difficult. But the city had been lucky. Further to the south, about 50 kilometers away the destruction was much more severe.

Leading one of the rescue teams was a young officer called Mansoor. He was not technically an officer yet as he was still under training. His superiors had decided that this would be a good opportunity for the young man to prove himself. He was known to be keen and eager, so he had been made the leader of one of the two rescue teams which had been assigned to check the collapsed buildings. The second rescue team was still being assembled and would start operations a little later.

Mansoor was a tall man, with a full beard and the air of an eager puppy. In his team he had a bunch of men some of whom were more than double his age. There were eight of them in the group and they waded through knee deep water to get to the first of the collapsed buildings.

Mansoor was in the lead. The team moved through the knee high water in the streets, approaching the ruined buildings. They held their equipment clear of the water. The team was carrying hand held two way radios for communication along with first aid equipment and stretchers. They were in touch with an air unit which was hovering above, ready to descend to pick up stranded survivors if necessary. Mansoor felt thrilled and full of confidence. This was the first time that he was leading a group of men in anything other than a simulated situation.

The first building they approached was an old textile mill. On the radio, Mansoor was directed by his Situation Commander not to spend much time at this site. All the staff was accounted for and safe and it was unlikely that there would be any customers who were still trapped inside.

Still, to be sure, the team circled the building, calling out and keeping their eyes and ears tuned for signs of life. Above them, the helicopter hovered, the airborne team surveying the area with binoculars. They were high and far enough to keep the sound of their rotors to the minimum.

Mansoor led the call, as the team waited outside the building. They called out for two minutes and kept silent for another two. For about twenty minutes they kept up the call, circling the building. Later, when the waters had receded and when there was enough time to take a more detailed tally of the local people, the search and rescue efforts would be intensified. For now they were focusing on getting any easily detectable survivors out of the danger area. There were rumors of aftershocks still to come which could cause further damage. Now was the time to do what they could before the situation worsened.

Mansoor completed his circuit of the building and signaled to his team to move on to the next one. This was a three story structure and it remained partly intact. The facade of the building had come down and was lying in ruins, blocking access to the building. But Mansoor could see that a good part of the second floors and third floors were intact, missing their front wall. He could see right inside the building. The first floor had been a coffee shop and there were reports of people being trapped inside. Mansoor thought that if they had moved back to the interior of the building there was a good chance that they were still alive. He hoped so. Not only for their sake but for his as well. He could picture the fame and glory that would surround him if he actually managed to rescue someone. Well, maybe not so much fame and glory but something that would certainly attract the attention of his senior officers and look very good on his record.

Mansoor's team approached the building. He briefed his men and they split up into groups and began to circle the ruins, calling and listening.

Chapter Six

Unaware of the activity taking place outside the building, Karan and Stella sat silently in the near dark, waiting. After a while, Stella spoke.

"There's something I have to tell you," she said

"What is it?" asked Karan, curiously. They hadn't known each other for more than a few hours yet the girl seemed to feel that he was a close friend. For himself, he was just anxious to get out of here. He was confident that they would be rescued; it was just a matter of time. But he suspected that Stella's injuries were much more serious than she realized and that she was in a state of shock.

"I'm not from the talent agency V-Spot. I'm not even a play back artist," said Stella

Karan gazed at her curiously. "Then why did you come to my apartment?" he asked.

"That's what I'm trying to tell you," said Stella, putting her hand over his. She spoke very softly and Karan had to strain to hear her.

"I'm a part time model," Stella continued "at least I work part time because I don't get a lot of work. I wanted to try and get a job as a singer. I was at the V-Spot agency on the day that you called and asked for a singer. I overheard the conversation and noted your address down.

I decided that I would try and contact you myself and see if you had something for me. And then I was there again today when they were trying to call you to tell you that the singer they had assigned to you had a cold and would not be able to make it today and they couldn't get anyone else. But they couldn't get through to you on the phone, so I decided to turn up at your flat and take my chances. You weren't at home and I was about to leave when you showed up so suddenly."

Karan said "I had gone to the beach for a walk. But why did you do it?" he asked.

Stella smiled at him and her face was sad. "I have to earn a living," she said

Karan studied her face. "You're not married," he said. It was more of a statement then a question.

"No," she replied, smiling wistfully.

"What about your parents?" he asked

"My parents died when I was very young. I am alone. I live in a hostel with other working girls like me."

Now she didn't look sad. She spoke in a matter of fact manner, as if resigned to her situation in life, just as she seemed resigned to the fact that she was buried under a collapsed building.

"What about you?" she asked.

"I'm not married," said Karan. "I had a friend, a girl, whom I grew up with. We were never romantically involved but we were close and used to see each other often. She died a few years back of an illness."

"And left you alone," said Stella

"Only after she died did I realize that I loved her. But what difference would it have made? She would have died anyhow and I would have felt a lot worse."

"Don't say that," said Stella, putting her arm on his again. It seemed strange to Karan that she was the one comforting him and not the other way around. "You can always change fate. Nothing is predestined."

Karan was surprised at her words. "Do you remember what you told me about your gift of prophecy? There was a tsunami today, remember?"

Now it was Stella's turn to be surprised. "A tsunami?" she exclaimed "I thought there was an earthquake."

"We were hit by both. Your prophecy was true but there was more which you hadn't seen."

"But it is always like that," said Stella, speaking excitedly. Karan glanced at the block of cement lying across her lower body. He wondered why she wasn't scared out of her mind.

"It's always like that," repeated Stella. "There's more to fate and destiny than anyone can really foresee, even when things happen to them. And I do believe that we have the power to shape our future."

"Maybe," said Karan. He was losing interest in the conversation. He wondered if the water outside had receded and if rescue operations had started.

The two of them sat in silence. Karan looked up at the hole in the ceiling and wondered if there was any way he could climb up there. He glanced around the ruins of the room and then at the entrance to the kitchen. Maybe if he found some rope, he could figure out a way to climb.

Next to him, Stella moaned. Karan glanced at her and noticed that there was a pool of liquid spreading around her lower body. He looked again in horror and then put his hand out and touched it. He brought his hand up to his face and saw the red stain on his fingers. He turned to Stella and saw that she was watching him.

"I'll never forget that you came back for me," she said. "No matter what happens, whether I live or die."

Karan got up to his feet. He was disturbed now and could not bear the prospect of the girl dying next to him.

"We should shout and make some noise," he said. "If there are people out there they will hear us and come to us."

"I don't have the strength to raise my voice," said Stella.

Karan threw back his head and let out a long yell. It was deafening in the enclosed space that they were in and Stella winced.

Both of them listened intently for an answering call, but they heard nothing. Karan yelled again and they waited. Still nothing. He uncapped the bottle of water and took a swig. Then taking a deep breath, he threw back his head and bellowed again.

In the resounding silence that followed, he took another sip of water and then held the bottle for Stella and supported her head while she drank thirstily. Faintly, far away, they heard an answering call. Karan and Stella looked at each other in shock and then Karan eased her head down and was on his feet again, screaming at the tip of his voice, long and hard.

Mansoor was at the side of the building. There were few windows on the ground floor and those that were there were closed. The whole place had been air conditioned and the sealing of the natural flow of air would dampen any sound, thought the young officer. Though of course the walls had fallen down now. Still, the sound was faint. He called out loudly and waited for a reply. It came to him as an indistinct sound, so far away and so weak that he automatically ignored it, till he suddenly realized what he had heard. He held his hand, palm upright, and his companion stopped. Mansoor yelled again and this time he heard the answering call distinctly. The army officer turned to his subordinate.

"Get the others! There's someone inside and we're going in."

He was excited. This was his chance. He let out another shout and then turned and headed to the front of the building. Using his radio he called his Situation Commander and told him that he had found signs of life in the building. The sit com guided the chopper to Mansoor's location and in a few minutes it was hovering above the building. Spotters inside the chopper informed the team below that from what they could see, the front wall and a part of the floor immediately above ground level had collapsed. It would be dangerous, they advised. The building could collapse at any minute. It was Mansoor's decision and if he did decide to go in, the airborne team recommended making a cautious entry by climbing up to the second floor and working their way from there to the ground floor. Any survivors would likely be only on the first two floors and possibly in need of urgent medical attention.

The rescue team regrouped in front of the ruined building and Mansoor led the discussion on how best to enter the building and conduct the search without unduly risking the lives of the team members. There was much discussion among the group which the young officer freely allowed and when they had decided on a plan, Mansoor spoke to the Situation Commander over his radio and briefed him on what they were going to do.

Inside the building, Karan was excited. They hadn't been trapped long, maybe three hours at the most and already rescue was at hand. He whispered a prayer of thanks and turned to Stella. Her face was pale and the dark pool of blood around her lower body had grown larger. Karan hoped the rescuers would reach soon. He did not think that the girl could last long.

He sat down next to Stella and took her hand. She smiled at him weakly. She began to speak but Karan could not make out what she was saying. He bent his face low towards her.

"When I was a little girl," said Stella, her voice faint and weak, just a hoarse whisper, "when I was a little girl, my mother took me one day on a pilgrimage. It was just a one day pilgrimage. We travelled by bus and then took a boat. Finally we reached a church which was by the sea side. At the church, my mother prostrated herself and then she got on her knees and prayed for hours. I remember her best that way, on her knees, hands clasped and a look of devout piety on her face. I could not understand what she was praying so hard for. I grew restless and wanted to leave but my mother would not stir. Finally, we left and on the journey back, my mother told me that she had been praying for me. She said if anything happened to her, I would be looked after."

Karan could not meet her eyes. "You'll be fine," he mumbled.

"No," she said, "you don't understand. I am dying and I know that you know it too." Karan shook his head, avoiding her eyes.

"But I feel no pain, I feel like I'm going home," said Stella. Karan could see a tear trickling down her eye but there was a smile on her face.

"About three years after we went to that church by the sea shore, my father died and then my mother. Before she died she told me that she had known this would happen. That was the reason she had taken me to that church by the sea that day. I hardly remembered the trip till she mentioned it. She also said that she had a gift for me which would come to me when she died. It was not money or land or possessions but something much, much more special. I could not understand what she was talking about and I thought that it was the illness which had affected her mind. Then she died and I was sad and alone but I was not scared or lonely, somehow."

Karan moved his hand up on to her wrist. He tried to feel her pulse; it was too weak to distinguish. He moved his hand back to hers again and clasped it firmly. She wrapped her fingers around his hand and squeezed tightly.

"I was taken to an orphanage. It was a little unsettling at first, but then it got better. I was treated well, as were the other children there. The nuns who ran the orphanage took care of us and educated us. I studied hard."

Karan looked up. The rescue team was calling again. He yelled back and then he could hear them shout that they were on their way. Or words to that effect. He turned his attention back to Stella. He could sense that she had something she wanted to tell him.

"Unfortunately for me," Stella continued "or fortunately, maybe, I chose to study music. I could sing well and was chosen for the school choir. I dreamt of being a singer. But my teachers found that I could not sing solo. I could only sing back up or in a chorus. Although my voice could hit all the notes, I could not start till I had a prompt. I was determined to be a singer and maybe someday even write my own music so I persisted. I found I could sing using headphones. After I finished school I left the orphanage. The nuns wanted me to take up a job nearby but that would have meant giving up my dreams. So I came to the city and I've tried to make my way here. Then today happened and I met you."

"How long have you been here in the city?" asked Karan.

"Just about three months," said Stella.

"Well, you will have plenty of time to chase your dreams," said Karan. "We'll soon be out of here."

She moved her hand to his shoulder and tugged at him.

"Karan," she said softly, the tears flowing freely down her face now. It was all he could do not to look away from her. "I won't leave this building alive."

"Nonsense," said Karan, trying to speak confidently but his heart ached. "You'll be fine."

She tugged urgently at his shoulder again.

"Karan," and this time he held her gaze. Her eyes were soft and damp.

"Kiss me," Stella whispered urgently

He held her gaze a little longer and then bent and pressed his lips against hers. He could feel her soft, cool flesh and then her lips parted and they kissed for a while. When he moved his head away she caught his neck and pulled him down to her so that her lips brushed his ear.

"Because you never left me, and because I will be the one to leave you, I will bequeath you the gift that I have," she whispered in his ear and then kissed his cheek gently and let him go.

Karan sat up and found to his surprise that his heart was beating fast and his eyes were damp, like Stella's. He was about to say something when they saw a flash of light above them and heard a deafening yell, "HELLOOOO!"

Karan jumped back and shouted in reply. The voice asked how many they were and Karan replied and then the disembodied voice asked if anyone was injured. Karan told them to bring a doctor and a stretcher and people to move away the fallen masonry. The reply came quickly. They would be there in about twenty minutes.

Karan turned to Stella and put his hands around her.

"Hold on, Stella," he said. "They will be here soon and we'll get you to a hospital." Stella coughed. She put her hand to her mouth and coughed again. Little specks of blood sprayed on to her hand and she coughed a third time and now there was a fine sheen of blood on her hand.

"Don't leave me, Stella," said Karan and his voice betrayed his despair.

She didn't reply and his voice reverberated among the ruins. He had a horrible feeling of déjà vu. He had experienced this before.

A long time ago, when he was at that cusp between boyhood and manhood, his closest friend had been a young girl called Maya.

She was his neighbor and they had grown up together. He felt he knew her too well to ever think about her that way but she was annoyed that he didn't seem to notice when she grew up and became a woman. Still, they remained friends and went out together and had many things in common. And then she got the coughing illness and he was in the hospital with her, watching her cough up blood, and cursing himself for the fool he had been. He watched her turn from a young, vivacious girl to a tired, old woman in a few months and in the end he prayed that she would have a swift and merciful death. And he was there when she coughed up blood for the last time and smiled at him sadly and then turned her face away. A little while later she was dead. A small part of him died with her and he felt more alone then he had ever felt in his life.

After that day he could never take his emotions seriously. He wasn't about to start now.

With his arms around Stella, Karan yelled to the rescue team to hurry. They replied and he knew they were close by. He watched the hole in the ceiling while Stella rested her head against his chest and coughed, more frequently now. Blood spattered his clothes. At last, Karan saw the flash of light again and then it was gone and after a while it shone again and it was steady now and Karan began to pray as Stella began to convulse in his hands.

Suddenly a bearded face popped up through the hole.

"How many of you?" he yelled, his voice deafening, like a roll of thunder in the confined space.

"Two," screamed Karan "Get a doctor. Quick."

"Hold on," said Mansoor. He shone his light on them and then he ducked back. Soon a rope came snaking down and after a while the young officer slid down the rope. He was followed by two other men. They glanced at Stella and at the stone lying over her lower body. While Karan held Stella tight, the men strained together and lifted the rock. Stella moaned and then was still. When her legs were clear, Mansoor shone his torch on Stella and Karan saw that her legs were crushed and her lower body was drenched in blood.

"Where is the doctor?" Karan snarled.

"The medic is on his way," said Mansoor. He spoke tersely into his radio and then looked around.

"Is there anyone else here?"

Karan looked down at the young girl who lay ominously still next to him.

"No," said Karan," there were just the two of us." He cradled Stella's head in his hands and looked at her eyes. He kissed her on the lips and with the palm of his hands, gently closed her eyes.

"Now there's just me" he said, looking up at the army team, Stella's lifeless body in his lap.

****

The tsunami had died. The huge plates at the crust of the earth settled, nanometer by nanometer. The ocean relinquished the land it had temporarily claimed. The world continued its eternal wobble around its own axis. Comets and meteors hurled through space. The earth was calm. But it wouldn't be long before nature was unleashed again. Deep in the earth's crust the plates continued their slow, inexorable movement. The next collision and resulting chaos was inevitable. It was only a question of when and where. And who would be devastated.

****

Chapter Seven

Stella's body was placed in the ambulance and the doctor after noticing Karan's glazed eyes and exhausted demeanor, persuaded Karan to get in too. Her body was covered with a white sheet. Karan sat in the ambulance, on one side of the corpse. He put his head in his hands, partly to avoid having to gaze at the lifeless body of someone who such a short while ago was so full of life. He felt tired and sad. Just this morning his main concern in life was to compose a stupid jingle and earn his rent. Now he didn't think he would care about anything in the world ever again. He rubbed his eyes wearily. Across him, a nurse sat, studying him. Seeing the despair on Karan's face she came over and sat next to him.

"Was she very close to you?" the woman asked. She was middle aged, probably a good mother and probably an excellent nurse as well.

"I hardly knew her" said Karan. "we were just having coffee together when the earthquake struck"

"Life is strange" said the nurse. "You can't escape your destiny, no matter what."

That was not what Stella believed, thought Karan. He didn't reply and the nurse sensing his mood, kept silent.

Karan thought about what Stella had told him, the gift of prophecy that her mother had pleaded for her and presumably the same gift that she had wanted to give him. He supposed that she had been delirious and did not know what she was talking about. It did not seem that way at the time but her words made no sense, the more he thought about them.

The ambulance came to a halt and the rear doors were flung open. Orderlies climbed into the vehicle and Stella's body was taken away. The nurse led Karan out of the van and he was taken to an emergency center where a doctor inspected him and found nothing wrong. He was advised to rest for a few days and avoid stress and to see a doctor if he felt any kind of psychological trauma. Then he was told he could go.

He turned to the nurse who had accompanied him in the ambulance. "What about the body?" he asked.

She shook her head. "You are not a relative so they cannot turn the body over to you. In any case they will do an autopsy, maybe tomorrow, and wait for her relatives to come."

"She doesn't have anyone," said Karan.

"Then she will be taken care of by the hospital and the City. You can come back tomorrow and ask about claiming the body if you wish. Why don't you go home and get your wife to give you a good meal?"

"I don't have a wife," Karan growled

"Your mother, then," said the nurse

"She lives a hundred miles away."

"Don't you have anyone you can talk to?"

Karan looked back over his shoulder towards the place where they had taken Stella's body. "No" he said.

Mansoor watched as the team of stretcher bearers took Stella's body away to the waiting ambulance which was parked several hundred meters away, in the dry section of the road. Another of Mansoor's team walked with Karan to the ambulance. Strange couple, he thought. He had the odd feeling that something had happened there in the collapsed building.

Mansoor waited till the ambulance drove away. Once it was out of sight, he turned to his team.

"Come on," he beckoned, shepherding them forward with his arms. "We've got more work to do."

They continued their search of the buildings. Next to the restaurant there was another building which had partly collapsed. Mansoor decided to lead his team in. This time he didn't ask for any kind of risk assessment form the helicopter unit. Once he and his men were inside the building, Mansoor informed SitCom over the radio that they were continuing the search. SitCom was not pleased. Mansoor was supposed to clear it with him before he exposed his men to any kind of danger. But he was doing a good job so far and the SitCom, a senior army officer, decided to let the young man have his way.

"Do you need backup, Unit One?" SitCom asked

"Negative," Mansoor replied into his handheld radio. "Just tell those guys who've gone to the ambulance to catch up with for us."

The team began to call and wait for a response. Almost immediately they heard a woman's voice, screaming in fear and panic.

Mansoor signaled for the men to stop and then he called out again. This time the woman's voice was clearer, pleading, lamenting.

They were in the first room of the building and as they moved forward again cautiously, they tried to determine the location of the sound. As with the previous building where they had rescued Karan, this building too was partly collapsed.

"Behind that," said one of Mansoor's team, a burly man even taller than Mansoor. He indicated a pile of rubble. Now they could hear the woman's voice clearly. She was crying out and sobbing at the same time. Mansoor raised his voice and called out that they were her and would have her out in no time. He and his team quickly began moving the stones. It was hard work and they called in the men who were waiting outside. Finally after about two hours they had cleared a path through the fallen stones and Mansoor crawled in with a flash light. He found a woman and a young child, both clutching each other in fear. Next to them was the still body of a man. Mansoor radioed the Sitcom and back up was sent. After another hour's work, the woman and child were led out of the building and the man's body was carried out.

Mansoor was advised by headquarters to take a break but he refused. He and his team kept working and now they were joined by a second unit who worked separately under a different team leader. Mansoor was not happy that someone else was also in charge here but there was nothing he could do about it. They found more people and in all they pulled out five live bodies from the ruins and four still ones.

It was late in the evening and all the squad had their flashlights out. They were tired and weary and ready to go back to take a well deserved rest. But Mansoor wanted to investigate one more building. The Second Unit had rescued four people and was still working. As they had started later than Mansoor's team, they would continue to work when he and his team had pulled back. But Mansoor wasn't happy with the other team leader rescuing more people than him.

Overriding the objections of his team, he led them into the last building. This building looked intact from the street but the rear walls had collapsed, leaving it exposed from the back. Mansoor and his team climbed up the staircase slowly, stopping at every floor to peer over the rubble to see if there was anyone there. They could see no one. There was no reply to their calls. Mansoor almost decided to turn back but he kept climbing. Finally on the fifth floor they found that although most of the floor was intact, the roof had fallen down in the middle of the floor. Mansoor climbed over the rubble, indicating to his men to stay where they were.

That was when he saw it. A black cat streaked across the floor on the other side of the rubble and Mansoor, following the motion of the cat, saw a prone figure huddled on the floor. Just a few feet from the figure, the floor vanished and a huge hole gaped. Mansoor called his men up to the top of the rubble and they had a hurried conference. The figure lay still but may still be alive, though injured. If they approached the figure, there was a chance that the floor could collapse further, taking both the injured man and the rescue team down. They should radio the Sitcom and tell them what they had found. Perhaps a second team could somehow make their way up through the hole after buttressing the floor, and then rescue the injured man. Besides there was a good chance that the man was already dead in which case evacuating the corpse was not a high priority.

Mansoor overrode their argument. He chose the smallest man among the team, a young soldier called Vijain. Grabbing a coil of rope he gave it to Vijain.

"Crawl over there on your belly and tie the rope around the causality. Then come back and we'll pull the victim clear."

"But, sir," protested Vijain.

"Move it," snapped Mansoor.

Unhappily, the young shoulder slung the coil around his shoulder and began to crawl toward the victim. There were angry mutterings from the rest of the crew but Mansoor was impassive.

Vijain moved inch by inch towards the prone figure. He was terrified and began to sweat. The prone victim lay just a few feet away from the gaping hole in the floor. The young soldier tried not to imagine how far he would fall if the floor collapsed. Fighting his fear, he forced his arms and legs to move, pushing his body across the floor.

Mansoor and the rest of the team watched, holding their breath. Vijain seemed to move with agonizing slowness. The whole floor in this area was canted downwards. It seemed to Mansoor that it leaned even further over the opening as Vijain moved forward. Suddenly, there was a loud retort. Vijain froze, rooted to the spot. The rest of the team jumped up. One of the soldiers pointed to a large crack which snaked across the floor toward where Vijain hugged the ground.

"Come back," some of the team began to call out but Mansoor soon shushed them.

"Go on" he called out to Vijain. "It's nothing, go on"

But Vijain remained where he was, unable or unwilling to move.

"Come on, Vijain," Mansoor was pleading now. "Just a few more feet and you'll be able to reach the casualty. You can do it."

The truth was Vijain couldn't do it, even if he wanted to. His limbs had frozen. He wanted to turn back and scamper to relative safety near the team but he just could not move.

"He's frozen," said one of the team and Mansoor realized he was right.

"Shit!' he swore. He should have tied that rope around Vijain's waist before sending him off. Mansoor grabbed another coil of rope and tied one end around his own waist.

"What are you doing, boss?" asked a soldier.

"I'm going to fetch that clown," said Mansoor. "He can't move forward or back."

"Boss, the floor won't take your weight. You might tip it over"

"Stand back," he said angrily, pushing the soldier away. He got on his arms and knees and then fell on his stomach. Moving swiftly he began to crawl toward Vijain, cursing the immobile soldier.

When he was few feet from his subordinate, there was another sharp retort. Mansoor looked up and slowly as if in a dream, he saw the crack spread across the floor, around Vijain and the casualty and reach the wall on the other side. Slowly that area of the floor began to crumble. First the casualty fell into the hole and Vijain began to slide inexorably towards the opening. Mansoor lunged forward and managed to grab the soldier's leg by the ankle. At the other end of the rope, his soldiers hung on, digging their heels into the concrete and praying that the whole floor would not collapse. Now Vijain was hanging upside down over the opening. He began to scream. Mansoor could not gather the strength to pull the doomed soldier out and he felt his grip loosening. Vijain too felt Mansoor's fingers lose their grasp and he screamed louder and then his leg slipped free and he plunged five stories down to the ground below, his screams abruptly cut off as he hit the ground.

Mansoor screamed with rage and frustration. Quickly his team hauled on the rope around the officer's waist and pulled him back. When he reached the near side, close to the stairwell he sat up and cast off the rope.

"Quick" he said, jumping to his feet. Let's get to the ground floor."

Mansoor led the charge down the stairwell. When they reached the lowest floor, they found Vijain's body lying next to the body of the casualty. His neck was broken. Mansoor knelt next to him and felt for a pulse. But he knew it was a waste of time. He moved his hands wearily to his face and rubbed his eyes hard.

"Call it in," he said, feeling exhausted.

Sit Com dispatched Rescue Team 2 to the building. The team leader had instructions to relive Mansoor of his command and dispatch the rest of team one back to the base to rest and to be debriefed. Mansoor was to be placed under arrest and handcuffed. He was to be escorted to the base under armed guard.

Team Leader of unit 2 was a colleague and fellow cadet of Mansoor's. When he heard the orders he was stunned. He asked SitCom what had happened and was told that Mansoor had disobeyed orders and caused the death of one of his men. The Second Team rushed to the spot where the first team was waiting. Mansoor sat separate from the men, who were circling around, glaring at him and muttering to themselves. Team Leader 2, whose name was Rahul, quickly took charge of the situation. He realized that Mansoor's life was in danger from his own men. Quickly he sent the remaining members of Team one back to base camp. A stretcher was used to lift and carry Vijain's body. Rahul moved towards Mansoor and crouched next to him. He put an arm around the big man's shoulder but Mansoor angrily shrugged it off.

"I'm sorry," said Rahul "I'm really sorry."

Mansoor didn't reply and Rahul took the handcuffs from his waist and clipped it onto Mansoor's arms.

"Can you walk?" he asked

"Yes," Mansoor said, holding out his hands and struggling to his feet. He looked around him defiantly. One of his men who was moving away from the site turned and looked his former leader in the eyes. Turning to the side, the soldier spat on the ground and wiped his lips with the back of his hand. Mansoor glared at him, hate pouring from his eyes.

Rahul signaled his men and two of them approached Mansoor. One of the men placed his hand on Mansoor's arm, but he shrugged it off and began to walk. There would be no glory for him.

Chapter Eight

Mansoor was in the army court, awaiting the verdict his trial. Since had been taken back to the base, he had been held in custody till the trial began. It was all kept secret because the army was having a public relations problem. They had released a photo of Mansoor and his team which was actually taken before the tsunami. The local and even national papers had published it and proclaimed Mansoor a hero for organizing the rescue of five people from the ruins. The army insisted that they had been just doing their job but the media had been hungry for news and had quickly published the story, praising Mansoor.

Now in the event that he was found guilty, which was likely, they would have to face the probability that the rest of the story would come out. How Mansoor was guilty of insubordination and had caused the death of one of his men due to his carelessness. The only good thing from the army's point of view was that Mansoor was not talking to anyone. He kept absolute silence, speaking only when he was asked a direct question. His answers would come in short bursts. He did not even talk with the court appointed army lawyer who had been deputized to defend him. As a result, when the prosecutor had summed up the case against Mansoor, the defense could only argue feebly that Mansoor had been acting in good faith and had not spared himself the hard work and risks involved in the dangerous rescue operations. He had even risked his life to try and save the life of poor Vijain who should never have been included in the team in the first place.

The three veteran army officers filed back into the court and everyone present tensed, waiting to hear the verdict.

The lead officer stood up and read from a sheet of a paper. We find the defendant guilty of insubordination and involuntary manslaughter. Due to the good record of the accused we recommend that he be sent to army prison for a period of three years and after which time he should be dishonorably discharged.

There was a collective gasp from the people seated in the front rows of the court. Mansoor's head snapped back as if he had been hit on the chin. He stared at the tribunal sitting on the bench with despair and hatred. Two soldiers approached Mansoor to take him away. The bearded soldier flung off their arms and leaped over the small wooden railings and ran into the aisle of the courthouse. There were screams and cries and general consternation. Several soldiers in the crowd tried to stop the young man but Mansoor violently pushed them aside and ran as fast as he could to the main door of the court room. There was an armed guard standing on duty outside the doors and Mansoor, hurtling through the doorway, flung himself on the guard and knocked him over. Sitting astride the fallen guard, Mansoor punched him repeatedly in the face and then unbuckled the soldier's pistol and hit him on the side of the head with it. Then holding the pistol in his hand he reached out of the court room building followed by a group of soldiers. There was an army jeep waiting outside with two soldiers sitting in it.

Mansoor ran up to it, waving his guns at the men inside.

"Get out! Get out!" he screamed. The soldiers hurriedly got out of the vehicle and backed up the steps of the building. Mansoor jumped into the vehicle and started it. He sped along the road to the entrance of the camp. The soldiers guarding the entrance had been warned and they pointed their guns at the approaching vehicle. Mansoor ducked his head and pressed down on the accelerator. The jeep shot through the barricade, breaking the cross bar. The guards fired at the vehicle but Mansoor was away. Laughing like a maniac, Mansoor sped along the country road.

The army base was several miles from the city and there was not much traffic here. He sped along turning into smaller roads and driving into villages. He knew it would be some time before the soldiers gave pursuit. They would first get in touch with the local police to set up road blocks.

After driving or about an hour, Mansoor was in a deserted section of the road. On either side were fields of paddy. Mansoor slowed the vehicle and stopped. He looked behind and found to his delight that there was a pistol and an army overcoat lying on the back seat. Mansoor grabbed both and then he saw that behind the seat there was a steel box. He opened the box and found that it was full of hand grenades. The former soldier picked up four grenades and stuffed them in the pockets of the greatcoat. Then he got off the vehicle and hunted for a large stone. Placing the stone over the accelerator, he started the vehicle again, keeping the handbrake on. He pointed the wheels of the jeep at the paddy fields. Taking a deep breath, Mansoor slipped the hand brake doff and hurled himself out of the moving jeep.

The engine roared and the jeep hurtled off the road into the paddy field, its front wheels sinking into the mud and its rear end sticking out in the air. The engine soon cut off and the jeep settled into the mud, green shoots of wheat poking up all around it. Mansoor laughed loud and long. Then he put on the overcoat although it was midday and the sun was blazing, as he walked along the road and he felt cool. To hell with the army, he thought to himself. He was a god. He had saved lives and he could take them back any time he felt like it. He fingered the two guns that he had ticked into his waistband. He did not have much ammunition but he did not need much. He had saved five lives and all he would need was five bullets.

Chapter Nine

Karan left the hospital and took a rick back to his flat. It was late afternoon now. He watched the traffic flow by and the pedestrians walking to their daily destinations. Life seemed very normal. Not very many people had been affected by the combined effect of the earthquake and tsunami, especially away from the waterfront area. Near the sea, peoples' lives had been wrecked and businesses ruined. He did not know how many lives had been lost but compared to the vast numbers of people who lived in the teeming metropolis, it would be insignificant. The large majority of the people in the city would continue their daily lives. Excepting those who had died or the people whose lives had been affected by nature's rage.

After a long, meandering drive, the rick reached Karan's apartment building. Only just before he reached his home did Karan pause to consider if the building would be still standing. It was not very far from the beach. In any case, he didn't have anything to worry about as he found when the rick drew up outside the intact building. Karan got out of the auto, paid the driver, not caring that the man was overcharging him. At least the driver had the will to survive. He entered the building, feeling a dull weariness. No one here knew that he had been trapped under a collapsed building for a few hours. He doubted if anyone would care even if they knew, apart from the novelty of the news.

Tired and caught up with pity for himself and sorrow for Stella's short life, he opened the door to his flat and went in. He peeled off his clothes and had a shower, spending a long time under the hot stream of water, trying to wash away his troubles. That worked only to a certain extent, so after stepping out of the shower, with a towel around his waist, he poured himself a large measure of whisky and sat in his living room, sipping at the drink.

He reflected on the tumultuous events of the day. Stella, he thought, exclaiming to himself. In and out of his life in a few hours and she had managed to turn it upside down. How could he go on with his daily life after what he had been through? Nursing his drink and musing in this way, Karan sat where he was until it was late at night. He had several drinks more and then heated food for his dinner. After dinner he had his last drink and by then the events of the day were a blur. His mind was numb and so was his body. He could not even remember the events of the day. All that he was conscious of was a four note tune which repeated itself over and over again in his mind in an endless loop. And he kept thinking about money. Not how much he needed or how to get it, just the concept of money. Images of large piles of bank notes popped up in his mind like annoying advertisements on his web browser.

By now it was very late and Karan realized that he was extremely drunk, perhaps more than he had ever been in his life. He finished his drink, determined to find oblivion in alcohol, and staggered to his bed. The young musician fell into the soft covers and the music played in his head and images of piles of banknotes flashed in his mind and he was powerless to push them out. He kept his eyes tightly closed, feeling nauseated, and after a while, he fell asleep.

The next morning when he opened his eyes he felt confused. There was something important that he knew he should remember but he just couldn't think what it was. He opened his eyes wider and focused on the ceiling above him, where the fan was turning slowly. Stella's face came to him and then the events of the previous day flashed through his mind. He groaned and shook his head. Rising slowly, he walked to the kitchen to prepare coffee.

He walked back to the front room, sipping his coffee. Opening the front door, he picked up the paper from the floor outside the door where the delivery boy had dropped it. He glanced at the headlines. "Tsunami and Earthquake hit the city" it screamed. The article described the scenes of destruction and terror. He skimmed through it. In the city alone, more than twenty people had been killed and further down the coast to the south of the city the death toll was much higher. A total of five buildings near the water line had collapsed, struck by the combined force of the earthquake and the tsunami. There was much other damage to property.

He leafed through the pages and came across a photo of Mansoor, smiling heroically at the camera, surrounded by his rescue team. Karan read about how the young officer had rescued seven people from collapsed buildings before a tragic accident had killed one of his rescue team. Karan put the paper aside and walked over to his balcony, carrying his coffee. Standing outside in the morning air, he tried to recall the tune that he had composed before Stella came. He remembered that he had noted it down, so he went to get his notes. Then he sat at the piano and tried the jingle. After a while, he had it down, including the words. All he had to do was record it. He got up and finished his coffee and went to change.

In the shower he thought of what he would do in the morning. First thing was to call V-Spot and arrange for another singer. This time he would arrange to meet her directly in the recording studio. He had to complete the job today and send it in to his clients or he would miss his deadline. As the water washed over him his thoughts drifted to Stella. Who would claim her body, he wondered. Probably no one. It would lie in the hospital for some time and then she would be declared a vagrant and her body would be buried in an unmarked grave. He thought about all that had passed between Stella and him yesterday. Abruptly, Karan decided not to call the talent agency. He would miss his deadline and lose his client but what the hell, he thought.

Karan got dressed and picked up the phone and called Mistry. His neighbor and friend answered at the first ring.

"My man," said Mistry "where were you all day yesterday? I tried to call you several times. You missed all the excitement."

"Not really" said Karan "I had more than enough excitement yesterday. Listen, what are you doing today?"

"Trading stocks, as usual." said Mistry "Why? Do you have any plans? And where were you yesterday?"

"Listen," said Karan. "Get dressed and come over. We have to go and bury someone."

There was silence and then Mistry spoke up "Are you serious?"

"Yes," said Karan. "I need you to come with me. It's important."

"Okay, bro," said Mistry, "I'll meet you in half an hour."

Mistry rang the door bell thirty minutes later and Karan let him in.

"Where were you yesterday?" asked Mistry accusingly. "You said you'd be home recording."

"Actually, I was trapped under a collapsed building."

"Pull the other one," said Mistry, his face twisted disbelievingly.

"It's the truth," said Karan, leading his friend to the living room. "Now sit down and listen while I tell you the story."

Mistry sat and Karan told him all that had happened yesterday. He left out the part of Stella's prophecy, but nothing else.

His friend listened with growing astonishment.

"Wow," he said finally when Karan was done "You really had an adventure. And it's terrible about the girl. Was she very pretty?"

"Never mind," said Karan. "Now I need you to come with me the hospital and claim the body. I want to see that she is buried decently."

"That's not going to be so easy," said his friend. "You say that she had no one?"

Karan nodded.

"Well, first we should find out where she was staying. Then we might get more information about her. The hospital is not going to hand over the body without asking some questions and the police will be involved as well as it is a case of accidental death."

Mistry took out his dairy and began to make notes.

"I knew you were the man to call," said Karan

"Well, yes, you are lucky that you know me. You haven't told me if she was pretty."

"Very," said Karan "Very pretty."

"What a waste," said Mistry. Using his phone, he accessed the Internet and searched for working women's hostel in the metropolitan area. After he had made a list of the numbers he started to work his way through the list, calling each of the numbers in turn.

Finally on the fifth call, he had some success

"Hello, hello" said Mistry, "Can you hear me? Yes, good. I'm calling to enquire whether you have a girl by name of Stella D'Cruz staying in your hostel. Yes, yes, yes, I'll wait"

Mistry signaled to Karan that this call might be the one. He spoke in the phone again.

"Actually, there's been an accident, yesterday's earthquake... oh, okay very good. Can you give me your address?"

Mistry wrote in his diary and then he put the phone down.

"That's it," he said "it's a hostel near the city market and Stella was staying there. Now we will go and talk to the warden and any of the girls who might know Stella. I wonder if she had any pretty friends."

Chapter Ten

They left the flat and took Mistry's car. Karan sat in front next to Mistry who drove expertly. Karan sat quietly, gazing out the window. In his mind the recurring tune of the previous night started again. Karan rubbed his forehead and his friend glanced at him.

"Bad hangover?" he asked

"It's not that," said Karan "I've got this crazy tune running through my head and I can't seem get it out."

Mistry glanced at him again. "You are suffering from Post Trauma Stress Disorder. PTSD, in short."

"What would you know about trauma?" asked Karan.

Mistry patted his friend's knee. "I'm married, remember?" He laughed at Karan's expression. "Seriously, you should take it easy for a while."

"I'll try and remember that," Karan grunted.

They drove in silence and then Karan said "I keep seeing images of large piles of banknotes in my head."

Mistry glanced at him again, wondering if his friend was losing it.

"What denomination?" he asked, to humor him.

"What do you mean?" asked Karan

"Were they 100 rupee notes or 1000 rupee notes or what?" Mistry asked patiently, slowing down the car to let a pedestrian cross the road.

"I don't know, but they weren't rupee notes. They had the words First National printed on them. And they seemed to be million dollar notes."

This time Mistry slowed down the car to glance at his friend carefully. "Did you say First National?"

"Yes" said Karan "Crazy name, isn't it?"

"You've not heard that name before?" asked Mistry, pulling over to the side of the road.

"What are you stopping for?" asked Karan "No, I've never heard the name before" he said, seeing the way Mistry was looking at him.

"First National is a large private bank which is going public on the share market today. They are having their IPO. Nobody gives it a chance, but I'm going to take a gamble on your dream."

Karan sat stunned. He watched as Mistry stopped the car by the side of the road and took out his phone. Mistry called his office and gave instructions to buy ten thousand shares of first National.

In the middle of the conversation, he turned to Karan covering the mouthpiece of the phone and asked

"You want a piece of it?"

Karan stared at him in disbelief,

"I'm broke, man," he said

"I'll lend you the money," said Mistry. "How much do you want to bet?"

Karan said the first figure that came to his mind

"Twenty five thousand rupees."

Mistry spoke in the phone again and then put it away.

"Done," he said, glancing at Karan again. He started the car and they were on their way again.

Karan sat back and let out a deep breath

"Wow!" he said "I had no idea that you were such a superstitious gambler!"

"I'm not," said Mistry. "I was considering buying the shares all morning. It's a safe bet, I think. Are you sure you haven't heard the name First National before?" he asked again.

"Absolutely," said Karan, who didn't know the difference between stocks and bonds.

"Well, we shall see what we shall see," said Mistry and they drove in silence to the hostel. It was a fifteen minute drive and Karan realized he could no longer hear the recurring tune in his head. He decided that Mistry was probably right and he was suffering some kind of stress reaction.

When they reached the hostel, Mistry parked the car by the side of the road and they entered the building. A security guard asked to see their ID cards. The two men handed them over and the watchmen inspected the cards and studied them suspiciously before he finally let them in.

"Must be a lot of pretty girls here," said Mistry.

They walked to where a sign outside the door said OFFICE.

As they entered, an elderly woman met them at the door. "Yes?" she asked, her tone of voice chaellenging." Can I help you?"

Karan replied "We're here to enquire about Stella D'Cruz."

"What is your interest in her?" the woman asked suspiciously, her glasses quivering on the bridge of her nose

Karan cleared his throat.

"Stella was one of the unfortunate victims of the earthquake," he said.

"I was with her when she died. Her body is in the hospital and I came to find out if she had any relatives who could come and claim the body."

The woman's face sagged and her whole body seemed to collapse.

"Stella!" she moaned. "Of all the people it had to happen to!"

"You knew her well, madam?" Karan asked softly.

"I was the one who interviewed her for admission here. You see," the elderly woman continued, both anxious and agitated, "We get a lot of applicants who want to stay here and we mostly accept only those who come with a strong recommendation from someone we know. We want to avoid having a certain type of woman living here, you understand"

Mistry stirred and Karan stepped on his toe before he could speak.

"Come with me," said the lady and she led the two men to a corner of the office where there were three chairs and a sofa placed around a small table. They sat down and woman took off her glasses and wiped her face again, this time with a large white handkerchief.

"I feel responsible for the girls living here" she said "So many of them are so young. And they are often a target for predatory males who would turn their heads with money and ruin their lives." Here she stopped and looked accusingly at the two men both of whom looked away guiltily.

"I was the one who interviewed Stella," the lady continued.

"My name is Charmina Vaz and I am the warden here. Stella came without any recommendation; she just turned up here one day. Lucky for her we had a cancellation that day and a vacant room available. Somehow Stella convinced me to let her stay. And I was always glad that I accepted her. Until now"

"Destiny, madam," Mistry spoke. "We cannot escape our destiny, no matter where we go."

"Yes, well, Stella's life was so short and she suffered so much. Do you know that both her parents had died and she had no relatives alive? But she was a cheerful, happy girl. Amazing for someone who had been through so much."

"What was her job, madam?" asked Mistry.

"She wanted to be a singer," Charmina continued," I remember she told me that. I think she was doing some kind of part time job to earn a living. It's not often that we get someone here who is chasing their dream. Most of the girls here are working hard just to send all the money they earn to their families back in their villages."

Charmina Vaz removed her glassed and rubbed her eyes with the back of her hand. Then she replaced the glasses and braced herself.

"The day that she came here was a bad day for me. My husband had been diagnosed with cancer. I have children who are still young. I didn't know what to do. When the test results came, the doctor called me and told me. He hadn't told my husband yet. I was terrified, both at the prospect of telling him and at the fact that he was probably going to die. I didn't know what to do. I decided to leave the office and go some place where I could be alone. I collected my bag and was about to leave when Stella walked in the door."

Charmina sniffed and stopped again to gather herself.

"It was just a few months ago. She was dressed the way she always is, in a skirt that went past her knee and a blouse. I was in no mood to notice anyone at that time and I was about to walk past when she stopped me. It was her voice that stopped me, actually. I can't describe it, it was soft, pure, like crystal tinkling.. She told me that she was looking for a place to stay. I was about to tell her that we had no vacancies but something about that voice held me back. I told her to follow me and I went back to my desk and she sat in front of me and I began to ask her the usual questions. I had been through this many times before but this time I was not listening to the answers, I was listening to the tone of her voice. I don't pretend to know much about music but when she told me that she wanted to be a singer, I knew that she was born a singer. I checked the room availability, hoping I could find a place for her and to her luck there had been a cancellation and there was a bed free. But because of that voice, so sweet and so, oh, I don't know, listenable, I suppose, and her gentle nature, I decided to reassign the rooms and I shifted her to a room with a girl called Meera, another girl who has a very sweet voice.

I told Stella that I could give her a room and she was grateful and then she asked me if anything was wrong because I seemed upset. Then I broke down and cried and told her about my husband's cancer. She told me very directly that the results were wrong, he did not have cancer and that he should redo the tests. I thought I had heard her wrong because she didn't say they might be wrong, she just stated flatly and with absolute certainty that they were wrong.

Anyway, I told my husband that he should redo the tests and he did and it turned out Stella was right. The doctor was wrong."

Karan listened intently to her story. He thought of what Stella had told him about her gift of prophecy. He remembered what she had said about giving him a gift. He turned to Mistry and wanted to ask him why the stock marketer had bought shares in a company just because he had dreamt about the name. He decided that he would see a doctor as soon as he could and get some kind of counseling for stress.

"The thing was that when Stella told me that the tests were wrong, I did not doubt her for a minute. I was so certain that she was right. And I was so happy."

In the pause that followed her long monologue, Charmina rearranged all the items on her desk. Then she looked up at them and her eyes were bright with unshed tears.

"I think Stella's roommate is here. She didn't go to work today. Let me check."

Charmina turned to one of her staff and told her to call Meera's room and ask her to come down.

She continued to tell them about the hostel and the charitable trust that over saw it when a young girl wearing old faded jeans and a man's rough work shirt entered the office. The moment she entered, something caused Karan to turn to the door of the office. The girl looked up suddenly and met Karan's gaze and for a few seconds they looked at each other, eye to eye. For a few minutes, Karan felt the world slip away as he gazed into the young woman's eyes. In the back of his mind he heard the same recurring tune that he had heard last night and again in the morning. And then he blinked and she moved and the music stopped.

"Ah, Meera" Charmina Vaz beckoned the girl over.

Meera approached them and Karan studied her. He noticed that her hair was not very well done; it spread in a great mass over her head and looked like she had run a comb through it in a hurry. Her face was plain, not very pretty and she wore no make- up, none at all.

"Meera, these men are hear about Stella," said Christina. "There's bad news. Stella died in the earthquake."

Meera froze in sudden shock and then she covered her face with her hands.

"Please sit down" said Karan and the girl sat, moving with stiffly like automation. She answered Karan's questions in the same way, with no emotion and he sensed that she was struggling to keep her composure. He noticed that she had a pleasant voice, a little deeper than the high range that woman usually speak in. Now there were overtones of stress in her voice.

Karan asked her to tell him what she knew about Stella. It wasn't much. She confirmed that Stella had no living relatives, at least none that she knew off. She had been a nice girl, pleasant and she was looking for a steady job. She wanted to be a singer but Meera said that she couldn't really sing as her voice was untrained.

Karan could confirm that. Stella had been a nice companion and very easy to talk to, said Meera. She tried to continue but could not stand the strain any longer and she broke down and cried. Charmina was crying too. Karan and Mistry glanced at each other and waited. After a while, the women composed themselves.

Mistry spoke up. "We don't want to make this more painful than it is. The thing is, Stella came to my friend Karan's flat to audition for a singing job. They went out for coffee just at the time of the simultaneous tsunami and earthquake. Both of them were trapped together under a collapsed building. Stella died of her injuries just before they were rescued. Karan and I want to have the last rites performed for Stella so that her spirit can rest in peace."

"Neither of you are Christians, I think" said Charmina, drying her eyes.

"No," said Mistry.

"Well, I will arrange it with the local church. Stella used to go for there for mass and the parish priest knows her."

"Whatever expenses there may be, we will be happy to bear the cost," said Mistry

"It won't be necessary" said Charmina waving her hands in the air as if to blow away his offer.

"She has her security deposit with us which I will use for the funeral expenses. The rest of her things I will give away to the orphanage. Now what do you require from the office to claim the body?"

Mistry explained that they would require a letter stating that Stella had been residing there and had no living relatives and that she, Charmina would conduct her funereal. It would authorize Mistry and Karan to collect Stella's body. The lady had the letter typed out and she signed it and gave it to Mistry. Meera sat quietly, listening and watching.

"Where do you work?" asked Karan, trying to distract the girl from her grief.

"I work at a call center," said Meera

Karan tried to keep the conversation going but clearly the girl was not in the mood for small talk.

Once they had the letter from Charmina the two men left. They told the women that they would be back to help with the arrangements.

Chapter Eleven

Mistry and Karan submitted the letter at the hospital and after filling in various forms and signing various documents; they were told that they could collect the body. Mistry phoned Charmina who arranged the hearse and coffin. The body was moved to the church as they had nowhere else to take it. The funeral mass would be held the next morning.

Later that evening, Mistry and Karan returned to the apartment. Mistry joined his friend for a drink before dinner.

"What a day!" sighed Karan

"Yes, well, a little better than yesterday, don't you think?" said Mistry "We haven't had a tsunami today."

Karan grunted. The two friends sat in silence, sipping their drinks.

Mistry took out his phone and checked the messages. He whistled loudly through his teeth.

"First Nationals' IPO sold out on day one" he told Karan. "That means we have made a profit already. Trading starts in two days. It will be interesting to see how the shares perform."

"How much money did I make?" asked Karan

"We won't know till the trading starts," Mistry said "Did any other image pop up in your head?"

"You really think that my dream had anything to do with it?"

"Probably not," said Mistry. "Just wishful thinking. Still if you do have any strange dreams, do let me know. I am a lateral thinker"

"I will," Karan promised.

They finished their drinks and then Mistry left for his flat. Karan showered and had dinner and then sat watching TV till he felt sleepy.

Before he got into bed, he thought of Stella once more and then, strangely, of Meera.

The next morning Mistry and Karan drove to the church. They were in a more serious mood and did not chat much during the drive. Mistry told Karan that he would not be able to stay for the full service as he had to get to the office. When they reached the church, they were told that the service would be delayed because the priest had gone to visit a parishioner who was ill. Mistry waited for a while with Karan and then he had to leave. Karan waited outside the church. He was feeling uncomfortable and wondered what he was really doing here. Stella was just a girl he had known for a few hours. He didn't need to be here. But he knew that he would have felt a lot worse if he hadn't come. He looked around and saw Charmina Vaz coming out of the building. She had come to call him in, the parish priest had returned and the service was about to start. Karan followed her inside and took a seat at the back while Charmina sat next to the coffin.

It was the first time Karan had ever entered a church. He glanced at the cross over the altar. He knew the story, but didn't believe the words. All around him were paintings and statues of saints. Karan wondered where Stella' spirit was now. She was free from the troubles and worries of the world but did she even exist anymore? He looked up at the curved dome of the church. He didn't really believe in God but sometimes he hoped that God believed in him. Maybe if he was watching over everything, he would cast his eye on this frustrated musician and send a little luck his way, though Karan.

The priest came in and the service started. Meera was there, standing on the other side of the aisle, along with a few other girls from the hostel. Her head was bowed down as if in deep prayer and she had a shawl around her head. Immersed in her thoughts, she looked almost beautiful and Karan watched her a long time. He knew she was not a Christian and he envied her simple faith.

The priest said a few words about how all men and women were part of God the shepherd's flock and how He would look after every single one. Karan wondered if anyone was even listening. There were just a handful of people there. Apart from Meera and the girls there were two nuns, and a few old ladies. The nuns were young, wearing white saris with a blue trim. They were on their knees, eyes closed and palms together. Whatever they were praying for, he was sure it was not Stella. His heart clouded over in despair and he looked out the window at the patch of clear blue sky framed there. A beautiful day in a cruel world, he thought.

Something the priest said caught Karan's ear. The eulogy was on love and life and the priest quoted:

> "Thou hast made known to me the ways
> of life
> Thou shalt make me full of joy with thy
> countenance.

The words are from the Acts of the Apostles, Chapter 2, Verse 28. Let us dwell on these words and pray to the Lord for the wisdom to understand life and the humility to find love."

With that the priest concluded his sermon.

Nice words, thought Karan. He was ready to be cynical but something caught in his heart. "Thou shalt make me full of joy..." There was an indefinable longing in his heart and he wished that he could see Stella again, in person. Was it Stella that he was longing for or was it the promise of joy that could come from outside him, from another person? He wished he knew and he gazed up at the roof the church as if seeking an answer which might be inscribed on the roof of God's house but all he saw was the damp patches on the ceiling where the rain had leaked though.

The service was soon over. The priest left the altar and Karan walked up to the coffin and looked down at Stella for the very last time. She looked peaceful and beautiful, he thought. If she hadn't come to his flat that day, she would still be alive. But that was her destiny. She couldn't change that, even though she thought she could.

The coffin was moved to the cemetery and slowly lowered to the grave. The priest said a few more prayers and then the body was lowered. Karan picked up a bit of soil and threw it over the coffin.

"Rest in eternal peace," he breathed. Then he said goodbye to Charmina and Meera and left.

By the time he reached his flat he felt tired and depressed. He sat his couch and picked up the paper. Leafing through the pages he saw a heading "Army officer absconds". He was about to turn the page when he his eye caught the name Mansoor. Curious, Karan read the article.

"Mansoor, an under trainee officer who was a hero of the rescue operation after the earthquake and tsunami just two days ago, was reported to have deserted his post. The young officer had been under severe stress after the gruesome work he had carried out in the past few days. He is said to have had an altercation with his seniors and left his post carrying guns and possibly hand grenades as well. A large man hunt has been started for absconding officer. The authorities have warned that the officer is mentally disturbed and may be dangerous. Anyone seeing him or having any information of his whereabouts is to report it to the nearest police station or army headquarters."

Below the article there was a photo of a smiling Mansoor with his rescue team. Karan realized that it was the same photo that had been published a few days earlier. Another victim of the tsunami, he thought. He put the paper aside and went and sat at his piano. For the next two hours he played for himself, enjoying the music and improvising the tunes and tempo to suit his mood.

He felt better after his musical session. Now perhaps he could do some work. First he called his client, the ad agency which had given him the jingle to write. When he told them it was not ready yet they immediately cancelled the work order. No amount of pleading by Karan would change their stance. He even told them that he had been trapped under a building during the earthquake, but they either did not believe him or were not interested in his excuses. Karan put the phone down dejectedly and wondered what he would do now. He did not have much money in the bank, not enough eat for the rest of the month, let alone pay the rent. He supposed he should look out for a regular job.

Chapter Twelve

Karan spent the day calling different ad agencies. All of them told him that they would contact him when they had a vacancy, thank you very much. Finally he swallowed his pride and called his old employer. After much discussion and haggling, he secured his old job at two thirds of his last salary. Starting from the first of next month, which meant that he would still have to find a way to eat amd pay this month's rent. Maybe he could borrow money from Mistry, he thought. Then he remembered that he had already borrowed 25000 rupees to buy stocks. What had he been thinking about? Shaking his head in despair, Karan went back to his piano and played all day trying to shake off his low mood.

Karan spent a lonely day all by himself. He had decided that he would give up his ambitions to make it a musician on his own, at least for now. Maybe sometime in the future he could try again but for now to keep from starving he would have to take a salaried job.

The next day was a lot similar. Karan wandered listlessly in his apartment. He called Mistry but the stockbroker was busy in his office and could not spare the time to meet up. Karan spent a lot of time at the piano again, composing a few wordless tunes and wondering what direction his life would take. He avoided having a drink knowing he would become too maudlin if he indulged himself.

He thought of Stella and the few hours they had spent together. He also thought of Meera, Stella's roommate, though he was not sure what his feelings about her were.

The day passed and he went to bed early.

He was fast asleep dreaming that he was a famous musician, known all over the country, when the phone's incessant ringing dragged him out of the depths of sleep. He blinked and stared at the instrument a while before he realized that he should pick it up.

"Hello," he croaked his throat dry.

"Karan," Mistry's voice boomed across the line. "What on earth are you doing still in bed? Did you read the papers?"

"No," replied Karan groggily, "what time is it?"

There was a pause. "It is almost 1030" said Mistry

Karan couldn't believe he had slept so long.

"The twenty five thousand rupees you invested in First National has quadrupled and is now worth a hundred thousand." said Mistry. "Congratulations!"

It took a few minutes for Mistry's words to sink in.

"A hundred thousand?" Karan finally squeaked.

"Yes," said Mistry, sounding very satisfied with himself. "Do you want to hold or sell?"

"Sell," responded Karan immediately. "Take out the money that you lent me and put the rest in my bank account."

"Done," said Mistry. "Now get out of bed and freshen up. I'm coming to see you. We're going to pick out a few stocks together."

"But I haven't had any strange dreams," said Karan, wishing he had a glass of water to drink. He felt confused.

"Doesn't matter," his friend replied. "Just get dressed. I'll be there soon"

Karan hopped out of bed, his mood suddenly buoyant. He had received a windfall of 75000 rupees. That would last him two months at least. And all from a crazy dream. Briefly he recalled Stella and her gift for prophecy. Then he put the thought aside.

Hurriedly, Karan had a shower and changed. He made himself a cup of coffee and sat with the newspaper. In the business section he found the story of First National and began to read avidly. The bank's IPO had been a great success. Karan read the article and was skimming through the rest of the paper when another article caught his eye. It was about Mansoor, the hero of the disaster rescue operations. He was now called a rogue officer and was still missing and believed to be heavily armed. There was intense speculation about his motives and his mental health. It was reported that the ex-officer's decisions had caused the death of one his team.

Karan was thoughtful after he completed reading. A hero turned villain in one instance and a zero turned winner in his own case. Life was strange, he thought.

Just then the doorbell rang. When Karan opened the door, Mistry walked in, a sheet of paper in his hands.

"We've got some important work to do," said his friend. He grabbed the coffee mug from Karan's hand and drained it. "Ahh!" Mistry said, smacking his lips. "Now what I want you to do is go over this list of companies and pick any three that you fancy"

He handed the paper to Karan who glanced at it.

"What do you mean?" asked the musician. "You want me to choose three names at random? Why?"

"Just an experiment" said Mistry. "We'll see how prescient you are. Choose three."

Karan ran his eye over the names. They were mostly all unfamiliar to him expect a few big companies whose names he had come across in advertisements or whose products were household names. There was nothing in the names that he could differentiate. Trying to keep his mind clear, he ran his eye through the list of names. Still nothing. Karan took a deep breath, several deep breaths till his mind was calm again. He placed his finger over the column of names and slowly moved it down. As his finger scrolled down the names, he heard in his mind the now familiar tune. He stopped and moved his finger back up the list of traded companies, waiting for the tune to become stronger. At last he stopped at one name. The tune was clear and strong in his mind now. Karan looked up at Mistry who was holding his breath.

"Nature Foods," he said, reading the name out aloud. Misty nodded his head, waving at him to keep going. The tune faded in Karan's head. He resumed scrolling down the list and when the tune recurred he paused. He read out the second name. Garware Developers. And then the third. Spore Infra. Karan took his finger off the paper and exhaled in relief.

"Those three," he told Mistry, leaning back and rubbing his forehead.

Mistry pulled a pen from his pocket and grabbed the sheet back from Karan. He circled the three names Karan had read out.

"Nature Foods, Garware Developers and Spore Infra" the stock broker read aloud. "Now let's see what we can find out." He pulled out his phone and called his office. Speaking crisply, he read the names out to the person on the other end and told him to call back with a detailed report on the companies. Then he hung up and sat down on a chair. Karan sat next to him and Mistry reached in his pocket and pulled out a check. He handed it to his friend.

"Here's a check for the shares you sold plus a commission for recommending them."

Karan saw that the check was for eighty thousand rupees. He whistled.

"That was easy money," he said

"Easier than you know." said Mistry "Now we're going to find out whether you were just lucky once or if you are really lucky all the time."

"I wouldn't bet on it," cautioned Karan

"I would," said Mistry. "And what I'll do for you is I will invest your commission into the stocks that you have picked. That is 5000 rupees per stock."

"You're really free and easy with your money, aren't you?" said Karan. "Your wife must be very happy."

"You wish!" his friend replied. "And so does her. I made a huge killing on First National, thanks in part to you so I can afford to take a risk here. Besides, something tells me that you may be the lucky one"

"What is that something?" asked Karan

"Stella," said Mistry and Karan was quiet.

"I made some enquiries about her and what I found was enough to convince me that she was someone special. And I do believe that may have rubbed off on you because you were with her when she died."

Karan did not say anything for a while. After considering for a few minutes, he decided to tell his friend about Stella's belief in her gift of prophecy and how she had told him that she would give him the gift. When he had finished, it was Mistry's turn to be silent.

"Something in that," said the stock broker at last

"You really believe all that?" asked Karan surprised.

"What I know is that I made a small fortune investing in a stock that you dreamed about." said Mistry slowly. "Today we're going to put your new talent to the test. After the office calls me back with some history of the three companies that you selected, I'm going to invest in them. This will be the test of your abilities. Or Stella's, if her story is true. We'll know quite soon"

"You mean, if the share price rises, I am a proven oracle but if it falls, I'm just a one hit wonder?"

"Yes," said Mistry.

"You're crazy," said Karan

"Crazy like a fox," agreed his friend.

"Come on" Mistry got up and stretched luxuriously "Let's go out and have a few beers before lunch."

Chapter Thirteen

That night, as Karan finished his dinner alone in his flat, he thought about the check that Mistry had given him. Eighty thousand rupees. It was easily the most amount of money he had ever earned in his life and it was for the simplest kind of work. Dreaming. He wondered if it really had anything to do with his dream or if it was just pure luck. He tried to recall Stella's face, but it was vague and fuzzy and he had to concentrate really hard to remember what she had looked like. It was easier for him to think of Meera. Was he seriously attracted to Meera? The surprising answer to that question was yes. As to why he was attracted to her, he couldn't say for sure but he knew he was. And he would see her again. First, he would resolve the question of his second sight. Mistry told him that they would have to wait for a few days before they would be able to discern any activity in the stock.

Karan went to bed, wondering what he would dream about tonight.

The next morning when he awoke, he went to his computer and logged on to a site Mistry had told him about. He checked the price of the three stocks he had picked. All of the stocks were up, even though the broader market had traded down. Karan sipped his coffee and stared at the screen. He couldn't remember what he had dreamt about last night but he was feeling relaxed and comfortable.

In the afternoon he got a call from Mistry.

"You've done it, buddy" said Mistry, his tone full of wonder and glee.

"What's it worth now?" asked Karan although he had a fair idea.

"Your invested commission has earned you an additional fifteen thousand rupees." said his friend. "Don't ask me how much I made because I am not going to tell you. Do you want to sell or hold?"

"Sell," said Karan "and buy these shares with half the proceeds." Karan gave his friend the names of three lesser known stocks.

The musician had spent the morning going through the list of companies trading in the open market, waiting for the music to play in his head before settling on a name. He could not tell if he was forcing the music or if it was coming naturally. Still, he had nothing to lose and a lot to gain.

When Mistry heard the names he whistled

"Are you sure?" he asked his friend

"No," said Karan, "but just buy them anyway" Mistry laughed, "okay. That's fifteen thousand investment from you plus another commission for fifteen thousand from me which I will invest for you and I'll bring your check for the remaining fifteen thousand tonight. I think we have something to celebrate"

Karan put the phone down. Now luck was slowly being pushed aside and he was beginning to wonder if he had some kind of innate talent in share trading or if he was really an oracle. Slowly, he cautioned himself. First he would play the stock market and see how that worked out. Next he would think about resolving where his powers lay. For now, he had two phone calls to make. One was going to be a very satisfying call to his employer telling him he wouldn't take the job after all. He was looking forward to his second call too, which was going to be to Meera, asking her if she would have lunch with him tomorrow.

Karan spoke to his employer and told them he wouldn't be able to accept their offer. He tried but failed to keep a note of triumph out of his voice. When he was done, he put the phone down and sat looking at it.

After ruminating for a while he picked up the phone and dialed the number of the women's hostel. He asked for Meera and waited while he was put through. After a while he heard her soft musical voice.

"Hello?" she spoke questioningly into the phone, her voice as sweet as silver bells. Karan's heart jumped on hearing her voice. The voice of an angel, he thought. He contained himself and spoke up,

"Hello, Meera, this is Karan, the guy who was with Stella when she died. Do you remember me?" There was a slight pause. She was probably wondering why he called, thought Karan.

"Yes, I do?" the voice on the other end replied questioningly. Heavenly music! Karan realized the palms of his hands were sweaty. He took a deep breath and decided to push through.

"I was wondering if we could meet today for lunch. I wanted to talk to you about Stella."

There was another pause, and Karan waited, feeling nervous and fidgety and wondering why. The he heard Meera's voice say

"Is there something more that needs to be done for Stella?"

"No, no," Karan stammered. "It's just that I want to know a little more about her and I thought you'd be the best person to ask."

"I was her roommate only for a few months," said Meera. "I don't know very much about her."

"Still," said Karan, pushing his luck. "I'd like to meet you."

Meera took a while to reply. Finally she said "Okay."

Karan exhaled quietly in relief and they made arrangements to meet at one o clock near Meera's place of work.

Karan put the phone down, feeling as if he had climbed a mountain and was now looking down at a beautiful valley that he would soon explore.

Meera put the phone down at her end. She remembered Karan quite well. When she had first set eyes on him in the hostel office she had for a brief moment wondered speculatively about him. He was a tall, well built, virile looking man and at first she had thought that he was a bit of a rake. But talking to him that day and later at the funeral she had come to realize that he was gentle and kind though perhaps a little insensitive. She had thought about him again later, in the days after the funeral and was surprised to find herself thinking that it would be nice see him again. She had put the thought out of her mind, sure it would never happen and now, out of the blue, his call had come asking her to lunch. Even though he had told her that he wanted to talk about Stella she knew from the tone of his voice that he was eager to see her and she felt light hearted.

Meera chose her clothes carefully. She donned a light colored churidar, pale green in color, with a matching shawl. She looked cool and comfortable. She put on some make-up, a little lipstick and a touch of eyeliner to add contrast to her eyes. Looking in mirror she wondered if she was dressing for work or dressing for her date. She added a touch more lipstick and smacked her lips, smiling a little to herself.

Karan spent the morning wondering about his gift of prescience and wondering if he was going a little crazy. How did he really know that the tune in his head was coming unbidden or if he was just recalling it. He checked the stock market rates but it was too early and there was no change in the price of the stocks that he had picked. He gave it up and moved away from his computer. Although he had plenty of time, he decided to dress for his date and choose his clothes carefully. He wasn't a sharp dresser and didn't have much of a choice in his wardrobe. He had to settle on a formal shirt silver grey in color and a pair of well pressed blue jeans. He wore a leather belt with a shiny buckle with the jeans and combed his hair carefully in the mirror. Karan couldn't remember when he had last dressed this carefully for anything.

With a final glance in the mirror, he left his apartment locking the door and pocketing the key.

Whistling to himself, Karan raced down the stairs and at the second landing he met Mistry puffing his way up, carrying a large bag of groceries.

"Mistry," Karan laughed "you look miserable. Why don't you take the lift?"

"Staying fit, you twerp," said his friend "and where are you off too dressed like that?"

"Got a date, buddy," said Karan, racing down the stairs past his friend

"You lucky dog," said Mistry watching his neighbor run down the stairs. "I bet she's pretty," he said wistfully.

"They all are, Mistry, they all are. You just need to know how to bring it out in them." Karan yelled up the stairs.

Mistry watched him go, shaking his head, and then resumed trudging up the stairs.

He wondered if Karan was having a nervous breakdown of some kind. Of course, he didn't look like he was suffering from anything but Mistry knew enough about stress to understand that it manifested itself in strange ways. The stockbroker had been humoring his friend, trying to keep his mind off the tragedy that he had experienced. What he was worried about was that Karan would really begin to believe that he had foresight. Mistry shrugged to himself and took out his smart phone. As he was climbing he checked the activity on the stocks that Karan had picked. He saw that all the three stocks had moved significantly upward in the last fifteen minutes and then he asked himself why he wasn't surprised. Maybe he was the one who was suffering from stress.

Karan waited at the restaurant for Meera, ordering cool lemonade and browsing through a paper he had found on the table. It was the previous day's issue and he glanced at it perfunctorily, leafing through the pages. An article caught his eye. The headline read "Hero or Zero, the strange experience of a military man" It was about Mansoor. Karan read the article.. It described how the young soldier had been convicted by a military tribunal of insubordination and negligence which had caused the death of a fellow soldier during the rescue of the victims of the tsunami and earthquake. The army had ordered an inquiry into the affair and it had not gone well for Mansoor. It seemed that the overeager officer had refused to call for additional help and as a result one of the men carrying out the rescue had died. He had been reproved by the tribunal conducting the investigation and had not taken it well. To put it mildly.

That same day, he had disappeared from the army base, after stealing grenades and hand guns. Now there was a second investigation going on to find out how the soldier had gotten access to the arms and ammunition and how he had managed to leave the army post carrying his weapons unchallenged. Meanwhile a manhunt had been started and so far had been unsuccessful. Mansoor had been heard to say that he would take back the lives that he had spared during the earthquake, which seemed to mean, the newspaper speculated, that he would hunt down and kill those people he had rescued during his mission. Karan finished the article, feeling a little creepy. Would Mansoor come for him? And if he could see into the future, if he really was prescient, would he have sufficient warning before he was attacked?

Chapter Fourteen

Karan put the paper down and sipped at his lemonade. From where he was sitting he could see the entrance of the restaurant and the road beyond. He kept an eye out for Meera, feeling a pleasant anticipation, tempered by a slight unease brought on by what he had just read.

After a short while, his patient wait was rewarded. A shadow blocked the sunlight streaming through the open door of the restaurant and Karan glanced up quickly to see Meera enter. The light behind her shone like a splendid aura surrounding her, her face was in shadow. And then she moved past the door and Karan could see that she was smiling at him. Karan stood up and waited as she crossed the floor and came to him. He took his chance to study her again. Not pretty but a certain charm, he thought, the way she held her hands close inside her body, elbows out her hips swaying gently, her slim figure crying out to be hugged. In her ice green dress she looked like a cool place in the shade, a shelter from the raging heat of the day.

She reached the table and before Karan could move a waiter materialized and drew back her chair for her. She smiled her thanks at him and at Karan again, and he waited till she was seated before he sat himself. She arranged herself, keeping her purse on the adjoining chair and settling her arms on the table. Then she regarded him, waiting for him to speak.

Karan was a little flustered. "Well," he said, struggling to find words. "It's been a while. How have you been?"

"Good," she said, coolly, but her smile was warm.

They talked about inconsequential things, Karan not really following the conversation but listening to the slow, sweet lilt in her voice. If she was not really pretty, her voice was a thing of splendid beauty. He wondered that she was not a singer, that no one had told her how sweet her voice was.

"You told me that you work in a call center," he said.

"Yes," said Meera, "it is not far from here," motioning with her hand across the street.

"Have you ever thought about being a singer?"

Meera laughed and Karan heard once again the sweet sound of bells chiming. "Like Stella, you mean? No, I prefer a steady job. At least I know I am going to get paid at the end of every month.'

"But still," said Karan, "has no one ever told you that you have an exceptionally beautiful voice?"

He looked at her earnestly and saw that she was studying him, her eyes full of amused laughter, her lips pursed as if to hide the smile that came to her lips at his sincerity.

"More than a few people," she said, "and especially my parents who made me take singing classes all through my school days. But I wanted some kind of financial security so I chose this job at the call center."

"Didn't Stella inspire you to take a chance?"

Now Meera grew serious. "No," she said. "In fact, when I saw how hard she tried to make it as a singer, I was glad of my own simple job."

"Don't you get tired of being screamed at over the phone?" asked Karan

"My clients never scream at me," said Meera primly. "I talk to them and they tell me their problems and I help them solve it."

"You probably hypnotize them with your voice," said Karan, but he was only half joking.

Meera laughed. "Like a snake charmer," she said

"Like a sweet charmer," corrected Karan.

The waiter approached to take their order.

Meera ordered a chicken broth and a plate of steamed noodles. Karan told the waiter to bring him a club sandwich.

They were silent for a while and then Karan spoke, "How long did you know Stella?"

"She had been my roommate for about three months, since she came to the hostel first."

"Tell me about her," said Karan

Meera regarded the young man carefully.

"Do you know that Stella had been in an insane asylum?" she asked slowly

Karan was stunned. All Stella's talk about her gift for prophecy now came under a new light. He even remembered that he had been convinced that she was crazy at first.

"Why was she there?" he asked softly

Meera looked down at the table top

"It was before she came to the city," she said "Stella told me about it. She had told the nuns in her orphanage that she could see into the future and they took her to a doctor who had her put in an institution."

"That must have been a long time ago, when she was still a kid," said Karan.

"Not so long ago. She was not studying at the orphanage at the time; she was working there with the nuns, teaching the younger children."

"And then what happened?" asked Karan. His heart was beating fast and he realized that he was scared.

She managed to convince the doctor that she had to leave the asylum to visit a dying relative. She told him that she would be back soon. And then she came here"

Karan was stunned. "You mean she came here after escaping from a lunatic asylum?"

"Yes," said Meera, watching him closely.

The waiter brought their food and they sat in silence while it was laid out. The waiter was a short dark man with a large stomach that protruded above the white apron that he wore. While he was serving the food, he speculated on the couple. Didn't look like a lover's tryst, thought the waiter. More like the girl had big news for the guy. He completed serving the meal and left the table.

Meera took up a spoon and began to stir her broth. Karan toyed with his sandwich.

"How many people know this story?" he asked finally.

"Only I knew it and now you do too," said Meera, "but I learnt to take everything that Stella told me with a pinch of salt."

"Why was that?" asked Karan, taking a bite out of his sandwich though he had lost his appetite.

"She used to say the most outrageous things," said Meera. "And she believed that she could see the future. She predicted all kinds of crazy things that never came true"

"Like what?" said Karan, feeling more and more depressed.

"Oh, all sorts of rubbish. Really, she was a sweet girl but I do believe that she needed help."

Meera ate her food and they did not talk much more till she had finished.

She spooned the last of the noodles in her mouth and only then did she notice that Karan hardly eaten.

"What's the matter?" she asked. "Is it not good?"

"I lost my appetite," said Karan

"Is it because of what I told you about Stella?" asked Meera perceptively.

"Yes," said Karan and then he proceeded to tell her what Stella had told him when they were trapped in the building.

Meera listened to him attentively.

Across the room, the waiter watched the young couple in silence. The man was trying to talk her into coming back to him, he thought. He could do better, the fat man thought. The girl wasn't so pretty. The waiter, whose name was Joseph was a married man but his marriage had no romance in it. He and his wife had been together too long and knew each other too well. But one thing that they both enjoyed was tracking the love lives of other couples. And one of the things Joseph considered among the few entitlements of his job was that he had the chance to observe many couples who would come into the restaurant for a meal or just for a cup of coffee. When he got back home he would tell his wife about the couples he had seen that day and they would speculate together discussing their loves life and their prospects, hoping that they would come again so that the progress (or decline) of their romance could be observed. Watching Karan and Meera discretely from a distance, Joseph felt a tug in his memory. He had seen the girl before and thought he knew what the problem was. She had another boyfriend.

When Karan finished his story, Meera thought a while. Karan had told her about his luck in stocks. After a while, she asked "Do you really believe that you have the gift of foresight and that Stella gave it you?"

"I do not know what to believe," said Karan and she could hear the confusion in his voice and felt her heart go out to him.

"Stella was a lonely girl" said Meera. "You must have come across as Prince Charming to her. She would have said anything to keep you with her."

"Prince charming? Maybe charming but no prince certainly. More like pauper," said Karan bitterly.

"Still," said Meera. "Listen to this story she told me once. We were talking about love and marriage, you know, the usual girl talk and suddenly Stella made a statement. She said marriage without love is like food without salt. I was surprised to hear her say that. I teased her a bit, then and asked her if she would marry only for love. She looked a little sad and then she told me this story

"Once there was a man who had the superhuman power to resist fire. He could walk through flames without getting burnt. This man fell in love with a woman who at first loved him back, but later when they were married she grew tired of him."

Of what use is your superpower? She asked him. I can bring diamonds for you from the center of the earth he told her, for he still loved her even though she did not love him anymore. Prove it, she told him so he flew to a volcano and dived into its depths. He swam through the molten fire in the heart of the volcano till he reached the depths of the earth. There he grabbed a fistful of stupendous diamonds and swam back up to the top of the volcano. But the intense heat was too much even for him and his body became incandescent. He took the diamonds to his wife who gasped at their beauty but did not notice that her lover was burning. He dropped the diamonds in her hand and then as he burst into flame, he kissed her, because even then he still loved her. She ignited and they both burnt together writhing in ecstatic agony."

Meera looked at Karan, waiting for his reaction.

"That's really a strange story," he said

"I think Stella knew that she would never find true love, like the man with superpowers in her story" said Meera "She is like that man and like him, when she found her love unrequited, she harmed her lover"

"But he did find true love," said Karan. "It was his wife that didn't find it. And do you think she harmed me?"

"She certainly seems to have caused you some confusion," said Meera, "so she did leave a mark on you"

"Sometimes I think Stella is now exactly where she always wanted to be," she continued.

"Where is that?" asked Karan, puzzled.

"At peace," said Meera. "No more striving, yearning, earning or having to wake up in the morning and struggle through the day."

Karan looked down at his coffee. The couple sat in silence, watching the shadows grow longer.

Finally Meera stirred. "I have to go now" she said. "I need to be back for the afternoon shift. Let me pay my share of the bill."

Karan protested but she insisted and he wished he had not called himself a pauper. Meera had given him plenty to think about but most of all he wanted to see her again.

"When can we meet again?" he asked her as the waiter collected their cash.

"Do you want to hear more about Stella?" asked Meera, standing up.

Karan held her gaze. "I want to know more about you," he said and he saw her spontaneous, warm smile flash across her face.

"Call me," she said and she swooped around and grabbed her bag from the chair and ran out the door, turning to wave at him as she disappeared past the entrance.

Chapter Fifteen

Karan walked slowly out of the restaurant, pre-occupied with all he had heard during lunch.

When he got back to the flat, he found a note from Mistry slipped under his door.

"Call me" it said. Karan dialed his friend's number. He wondered what if the call was about the stocks.

His friend answered and spoke rapidly into the phone.

"The three stocks you picked have made substantial gains" said the stockbroker. "I'm coming over right now. I want you to go through all the listed companies again and pick as many as you can. Focus on the names. I really think we're on to something here. I'll see you soon."

Without waiting for Karan to say anything, Mistry hung up. Karan looked at the dead phone in his hand and wondered if insanity was a communicable disease.

He went to his computer and logged on to a web site showing stock prices. He searched for the three stocks he had picked and saw that they had moved up almost ten percent, on an average. This was too weird, he thought. He ran his eye over the news ticker and saw a banner headline.

"Finance Ministry eases restrictions on foreign investments in the country". He read the accompanying article and realized that almost all the listed stocks on the Sensex had moved up as a result of policy changes announced today by the government. That explained it he thought. He just happened to be lucky. Next, he picked a few stocks at random and saw that none of them had moved more than a percentage point up. The songwriter did a search and found that excepting the three stocks he had picked, none of the other companies had moved up more than a few percentage points. Karan sat staring at the screen with a growing sense of shock.

Finally he stirred himself and picked up his phone. He dialed Meera's mobile number. She answered, sounding harried.

"Sorry," said Karan, "I know you must be busy."

"I'm not allowed to take personal calls during working hours." she said, speaking urgently into the phone.

"Just one question," he said. "Do you think I'm crazy?"

There was a pause at the other end of the line. Then Meera spoke "Listen, Karan, this is not the time."

"Just answer me," said Karan and there was another pause.

"No," said Meera "I don't think you're crazy."

"Because," said Karan "I don't think Stella was crazy either and I believe she had the gift of prophecy which she has passed on to me."

Before Meera could reply, Karan added, "and I think I'm in love with you."

Meera gasped and then she giggled "You ARE crazy"

"Meet me tomorrow, after work, at the same place," said Karan

"Okay," said Meera. "I've got to go now."

"Bye," said Karan, a strange peace settling over him

"Bye," said Meera softly, sweetly.

Karan put the phone down and ran his eye again over the listed companies, whistling softly to himself.

When Mistry came to the flat, Karan handed him a list of fifteen companies. The stock broker ran his name over the list.

"Are you sure?" he asked

"No," said Karan, "Listen, Mistry, you're an experienced broker. Do you really believe this is going to work?"

"I've seen it working, my man." said Mistry "Do you know how much the stocks you picked have moved?"

Karan sighed "Yes."

He was getting seriously confused.

"Okay. Here's a check for two hundred thousand and if you need any more money, just let me know."

Mistry took out his cell phone and called his office. He read out the names of the stocks and when he was done he put the phone away. He had a satisfied look on his face.

Karan studied the check his friend had given him. This was easily the largest single amount of money he had ever earned in his life. Yet he didn't feel as satisfied as Mistry looked. He did not really believe he had done anything worthwhile to earn the money. Still, it would certainly come in useful; there was no doubt about it.

Karan and Mistry went out for beer and after they both had developed a pleasant buzz, they had lunch. When the meal was over, Mistry leaned back in his chair and sighed with satisfaction. "This is the life!" he said happily.

The next day there was more good news. All the stocks that Karan had picked had done well and the frustrated musician was rapidly changing into a successful stock broker. Karan spent the day picking stocks, waiting for the music to spontaneously start in his head as he ran his finger over the names of publicly traded companies.

After he had sent his stock picks to Mistry, Karan prepared for his evening date with Meera. Once he was dressed and ready he realized he had not read the paper today. He picked up the tableau he had subscribed to and riffed through the pages. Buried inside a familiar name caught his eye, just as he was about to turn the page. Karan stopped and ran his eye over the headline again.

"Rogue army office threatens revenge" ran the headline. Karan read the article below. Mansoor had been termed armed and dangerous and a deserter from the army. His superior officers had described him as a highly strung young man who had been pushed over his limit by the accusations of negligence leveled against him by some of the families of the victims of the disaster. The army tribunal which had been investigating the matter had found the young soldier guilty. This was too much for Mansoor to take and he had absconded from his post, carrying weapons. It was reported that he had said that he would take back the lives he had saved. The article concluded with a plea to the general public to report any sightings of the renegade officer to the nearest police station.

Karan put the paper down. He remembered the tall bearded man who had pulled him out of the collapsed building. He had stuck Karan as a powerful but gentle man. What had caused him to turn violent? Even if he had been guilty in part of negligence, he had still saved a few lives. No one could dispute that.

It was time for Karan to leave now. He was looking forward to his meeting with Meera. Something there, he thought to himself. He wouldn't say he was in love with her but he did want to see more of her.

When he reached the restaurant, the same waiter who had served them the last time met him as soon as he entered."

"This way, sir" said the man with a knowing smile and led him to a table at the corner where Meera was sitting, sipping a fruit drink. She glanced up as he approached and met his smile with her own.

Karan slid into the chair that the waiter had solicitously pulled out for him. He glanced quickly at Meera, taking in what she was wearing. Sky blue jeans and a buttoned down shirt. Obviously, her office didn't have a very rigid dress code.

"You're early," he said.

"Yes" said Meera, "I managed to get away. Why don't you order something while we decide what to eat?"

Meera pointed at the waiter who was hovering nearby.

Karan told the man to get him the same drink which Meera was having. Then he turned back to the young girl. She sat with her elbows on the table, her chin resting on the palm of her hands. She was giving him a rather curious look, thought Karan.

"Is something wrong?" asked Karan, feeling a little disturbed by her steady gaze.

"There's something I need to tell you," said Meera, moving her hands away from her face and sitting up straight.

"What?" asked Karan, intrigued.

"I had a steady boyfriend for a long time," said the girl, her voice low and lilting.

"Is he still your boyfriend?" asked Karan

"No" said the girl and it was the sound of wind blowing sharply through a flute

"Then why are you telling me this?"

"The boy, or man, I should say, is someone you know," said Meera, her voice low and a little sad.

"Not Mistry?" said Karan, half laughing.

"No," said Meera "My ex-boyfriend is an army officer called Mansoor. Or former army officer, I should say."

Karan was stunned him "That's a coincidence," he said finally

"Yes," said Meera. "I spoke to him after I saw his name in the papers and he told me that he had pulled you out of the ruins and taken Stella's body out too."

Karan sat quietly, remembering what he had read about Mansoor in the paper.

"When did you speak to him last?" he asked

"That was the last time. I read that he had absconded from the army and tried to call him, but, of course, his cell phone was switched off."

"Why did the two of your break up?" asked Karan.

Meera looked down at the top of the table and ran a finger over the glass surface. "He can be a little overbearing at times," she spoke softly

"What do you mean?"

"I mean he's a bit too macho and dominating. I liked him a lot and still do but he needs someone submissive and I'm not like that."

"So the two of you had a fight and broke up?"

"Something like that," said Meera

"And how did he take that?"

"Not very well. He kept calling me incessantly, even at work. I had to block his calls on my cell phone. He got angry and came to the hostel to meet me in person. I refused to see him and he created a scene. Finally Charmina threatened to call the cops and only then did he leave. For a while after that I thought he was stalking me. But now I have not seen him for some time. Even the calls stopped."

"When was this?"

"About three months ago. I had no news of him till I read his name in the papers and realized that he was the one who had rescued you."

"How did he sound when you spoke to him last?"

"Full of himself, as usual" Meera looked away and her face was despondent. "He was very proud of what he had done but also angry because one of the death of one of his team which he was blamed for."

"That was what the inquiry was about. But what exactly happened?"

"I'm not very sure but I got the impression that he had refused to call for back up. And that he took unreasonable risks which caused the death of another soldier," said Meera. "The investigation showed that he could have carried out the rescue more safely if he had called for help. But he wasn't inclined to share the glory. He could have chosen to plead against the verdict. Instead, he went a little crazy. Mansoor was a little obsessive about his work and his reputation"

"How did you meet him the first time?" asked Karan.

"The army was having a kind of public relations exercise during which they opened up their base to the public for a few days. I went with a friend from work to see the base. Both of us did not anything about the army and we thought it would be a learning experience. Besides, my friend had a thing for men in uniform. We were walking around the base looking at tanks and armored cars and other stuff when I slipped and twisted my ankle quite badly. I was wearing these platform shoes which are really not the best for walking. I just didn't think that I would have to walk so much and anyway it was a last minute decision to visit that base. When the saw me sitting down and holding my ankle, one of the army men called Mansoor who was happened to be the only officer nearby. He came over with a first aid kit and bandaged my ankle. He did it quite expertly and by the time the doctor came, it was all patched up. The medic gave me some cream for my leg and then Karan helped me get a ride back to the hostel. Before we left he asked me for my phone number. I was still grateful to him for helping me out and he is quite a good looking guy. I gave him my number.

A few days later he called me. He asked about my leg and then he asked me out. We went out several times together and I wondered if it was getting serious. I began to like him, he could be very amusing but I knew that he wasn't really my type. And then one day he gave me a ring and when I protested he said it didn't mean anything but would I wear it just for his sake. I wore the ring and after that he seemed to take it for granted that I was his steady girlfriend.

Of course, I couldn't help feeling gratified at the jealous looks I got from the other girls at the hostel when he came to meet me there. But the charm wore off and one day I gave him back his ring and that was when he began to get annoying"

Karan looked down at the table and then glanced directly into Meera's eyes.

"How do you feel about him now?" he asked and his voice was more than a question. It was a challenge.

"I'm not in love with him. He was just a friend," said Meera. Her voice was strong and she held his gaze, till Karan looked away.

They were silent for a while. The waiter brought Karan's drink, a very satisfied expression on his face. He would have a lot to tell his wife tonight. The young lady had done right, telling the young man everything. Now it was up to the young man. Would his heart be brave? He place the fruit drink in front of Karan and wiped the table carefully. Then he melted in the back ground, taking care to remain within earshot.

Karan sipped his drink while Meera sat back and watched him. He had been stunned to hear that she knew Mansoor and had been his girlfriend even. It didn't bother him too much but now he was at a loss about how to proceed. He would have loved to talk about something trivial, maybe about music, though music could never be trivial for him, or movies or even plain gossip, just to hear her sweet, lilting voice. Karan was no longer interested in knowing more about Stella. Whether she had been crazy or whether she was sane didn't really matter. As long as he was with Meera. As long as she kept talking. Suddenly an idea struck him.

"You know," he said" I'm really a musician by profession and by nature. I have a few songs that I've written and I just can't get over how splendid your voice sounds. I wonder if I could record you singing my songs?"

Now it was Meera's turn to be surprised. "You think that I can sing? How do you know I won't turn out like Stella?"

"Stella had an incredible voice and so do you. I think that's what your warden, Charmina noticed about the two of you. You might have been soul sisters"

Meera laughed and now Karan knew for sure that his ears at least were in love. "Okay, I'll give it a try. What kind of songs are they?"

"Love songs," said Karan. "Are there any other kind?"

"Of course," said Meera, but she blushed.

"So that's settled then," said Karan. "You don't work weekends, do you?"

Meera shook her head.

"Okay. How about Saturday morning at my place? We can record there and see how it goes. If it works out well we will go to a professional studio later."

"How many songs have you written?" asked Meera.

"Lots," said Karan. "I never thought they would be any good but with your voice you can make anything sound beautiful!!"

Meera blushed again. "You haven't heard me sing yet" she said. "How do you know what my singing voice will be like?"

"I'm willing to take a chance on that" said Karan

They ordered food, the beaming waiter suggesting some of the choicer items on the menu. After they had eaten, they said goodbye and Karan left for his apartment, feeling very satisfied with himself.

Chapter Sixteen

Across the road from the restaurant, Mansoor, wearing a dirty overcoat watched the happy couple. He studied the young man and woman carefully. The woman was very familiar, he knew her well. He still felt bad about her, but he loved her too much to let her go easily.

The man was a different case altogether. Mansoor had saved his life and now he would take it back. After all it belonged to him now, didn't it? The watcher smoothed his thick beard by running his hand over it and cupping his chin. Then he felt under his coat for his weapons. They were all there.

He watched Karan leave the restaurant and walk toward and auto rickshaw stand. Mansoor darted across the road just as Karan climbed into a rick, quick enough to hear the address the young man gave the auto driver. Watching the rick drive away, Mansoor repeated the address to himself. He failed to notice the girl in the other rickshaw, going the other way, staring at him, exclaiming to herself in horror.

Inside the restaurant, the romantic waiter also saw and recognized the man in the overcoat. Life is sad, he thought, shaking his head at the futility of it all. He picked up the restaurant phone and called the police.

Mansoor slinked away into the darkness, melting into the shadows at the edge of the pavement.

The lights were still burning in the building where Mistry had his office. All the staff had left for home hours earlier, but Mistry still sat in his glass walled cabin alone, staring in disbelief at the computer screen. He just could not believe what he was seeing. Every single stock that Karan had picked had gone through the roof. Each of them had made a sizeable fortune now, in just a few days. Even though it had been a sort of game with him to start with, now it was getting serious. And uncanny. How on earth could Karan pick stocks like this? Could he really see the future? What else could he predict? Mistry shivered. He shut down the computer and prepared to leave the office. Before he went home he would sit somewhere over a quiet drink and think about the implications of this. He decided that he would meet Karan again only next week. He needed some time to gather his thoughts.

By the time Karan reached his flat, all thoughts of the stock market and share prices had left his head. He entered his flat and locked the door behind him apartment. Going quickly to his work desk he rummaged in the drawer till he found the music sheets he was looking for. He went through them and then rummaged some more till he had found all the music that he was remembered writing. They were songs he had written over the years, never actually recording them or even playing them for anyone. But he had a feeling he could do something with it now, together with Meera. Karan took the scores to the piano and sat with them. He played each song, singing softly. He made a few corrections and additions to each of them and when he was satisfied, he put them away. He could hardly wait till the weekend.

Lying in bed later that night he thought of Meera and her sweet voice till he finally fell asleep.

Back in the working woman's hostel, Meera sat alone in her room. She had not got a new roommate yet. She had bathed and changed and now she sat on her chair, looking out the window. The night was dark but from where she sat she could see a solitary streetlight casting its yellow light on the mango tree that grew outside her window. The leaves of the tree looked sickly and yellow yet she knew that in fact they were young and healthy. Appearances can be deceptive, she reminded herself. The shadow cast by the tree fell across the road and Meera could see there was no one around. She thought of Stella and sang softly to herself. It was a song of love and comfort, of loneliness and fear, of grace and solace. After she had sung for a while she thought of Karan and hugged herself. Could he be the one? She went to bed with the song still playing in her heart and a smile settling on her face.

Saturday morning Karan was up and shaved and changed all before seven, which was very early for him these days.. He had called Meera the previous evening and they had agreed that she would reach Karan's flat by ten. He had given her directions. She was not familiar with the area but she would call him if she had any difficulty in locating the place. Karan could tell that she was excited about the recording. He was too, but not just about the recording.

Now he frantically tidied up the flat as best as he could. After a short hesitation, he tidied up his bedroom too. Although he seriously doubted that anything of that nature would occur, he thought he had better be prepared. He wished he had thought of tidying up before he had changed into his good clothes.

At last he was done and he sat on his sofa, perspiring slightly from his exertions. He had a pot of coffee ready in case Meera should want some and in a rare burst of foresight he had even stocked up on fruit juice. He checked his watch and then got up and began to pace the floor impatiently.

It was five minutes to ten when the doorbell rang. Karan ran to the bedroom, checked his appearance in the mirror and then went to the door, smoothing his hair with his hand. When he opened the door, Meera stood there, smiling at him and holding a large packet of fruit juice.

"In case we get thirsty while we work," she said, walking in and handing the carton of fruit juice to Karan. Karan led her into the living room and poured out coffee for her while she looked around the flat. He noticed that she was looking fresh and pretty in a floral skirt and a pink blouse. It looked like she had put on a little more make up than on the previous day. He was flattered that she should take the trouble to dress up for him.

After they had both settled down, making a little small talk, Karan decided that he should keep this professional, at least for now. Meera didn't look very uncomfortable, being in a bachelor's apartment but somehow he was feeling a little nervous. Not that this was the first time he had a girl up her. Quite the opposite, in fact.

Karan walked over to the piano and collected the sheets of music he had written. He handed them to Meera who began to go through them

"I'll sing as well as play the music for you, so that you can catch the tune"

Meera looked up from the music sheets. "I can read music," she said

"You can?" said Karan surprised. "How come?"

"I learnt music in school. My father always wanted me to be a singer but I wasn't keen on it."

"Why not?" asked Karan curiously?

"Just because," said Meera. After a while she added, "I want to live a normal life, not the life of a songbird in a cage."

"You could have a wonderful life if you make it as a singer," Karan reminded her.

"That's a matter of opinion," said Meera.

"Well, anyway, if you can read the music that makes it a whole lot easier," said Karan. He walked over to the piano and sat on the little stool. "I'll just play the music and you listen and try and get a feel for it. Then we'll start again and you can sing along."

Karan played and Meera studied the sheets and began to hum along. When they had gone though the whole piece, Karan turned to her again

"Ready?" he asked

"Yes," said Meera quietly.

He played and she sang. When she started, Karan was so much overcome that he almost forgot to play along. Her voice was superb, both in tone and scale. The song seemed to shimmer in the air like sunlight over water, like light glinting off fine crystal, suspended in the air, the notes filling every corner of the room. The whole apartment seemed to be surrounded in a sweet, delicate cocoon of sound that lingered and slowly faded as Meera' voice died down at the end of the song.

"Wow!" said Karan. He struggled to find the words to express himself. "I cannot believe that no one has spotted your talent before."

He was excited, very excited. The girl had taken his simple song and transformed it into a piece of wonderful music. She was very good, no doubt about it. How no one else had noticed was a mystery to him.

"Well, their loss is my gain!" he said

Getting up from his piano stool, he moved hurriedly to prepare the recording equipment. When it was all set up, he said,

"Let's do it again".

He pointed at the blinking light on the recorder and then began to play. Meera sang and it was even better than before.

They spent all day recording, breaking only to have a quick lunch that Karan ordered from a nearby restaurant. After they had eaten and taken a short break, they continued recording. They worked well together, with Karan directing her and Meera suggesting a few changes in the music or the lyrics. By late evening they had completed recording all the twelve songs that Karan had prepared. The aspiring musician was ecstatic.

"This has been the best day of my life" he announced proudly. He pulled the recorded CD out of the tray and held it up in the air like it was a victory plate. "This is amazing," he said, enunciating each word slowly and carefully. "Truly amazing.

He brought the CD to his lips and kissed it.

"You are amazing," he said to Meera and brought her face close to his. Suddenly he froze, realizing he might be taking an unwanted liberty. He moved back and then he asked hesitantly "Can I kiss you?"

Meera laughed. She grasped the young musician by the ears and drew him to her. She kissed him gently on the lips.

"Come on," said Karan getting up in a burst of excitement. "We'll go out and have dinner to celebrate."

They went to an expensive restaurant. It was the first time Karan had ever been in such a place and he thought that Meera might be feeling constrained by the slightly stifling ambience, as he was. After they had ordered food he leaned across the table and asked her. "Tell me the truth. Why is it that you never wanted to be singer? You have the most amazing voice."

Meera said "I want to be a singer now. I never ever heard such beautiful songs as the ones you wrote."

Karan clenched his fist and pumped it twice in the air.

"But let me tell you a story," said Meera, sitting back and arranging herself comfortably on her chair. Karan sat back to listen. It was the easiest thing for him to do. He could have listened to her voice all night.

"There was once a mighty king who had a very beautiful daughter" said Meera "The king love his little daughter more than anything else in the world but when she was twelve years older he realized that she would grow up to be a stunning and possibly dangerously beautiful woman.. He began to fear for her safety.

The old king feared that any man who looked upon his lovely daughter would want to steal her away. He thought about this problem for a long time and his apprehension grew. Finally, after much deliberation, he decided that for her own safety and for his peace of mind he would lock his daughter away in a room in the castle with only her governess to look after her and teach her. She would not be allowed to go out and no one would be allowed in.

No one else would be allowed to see her. So it was done. The princess was locked up with her governess who taught her from books that were brought to the room. Meals were brought to her and the lovely princess was given everything that she could ever want or dream of except her freedom. Or a mirror.

So that the princess would not grow to be vain, the king had ordered that she never be able to see her reflection. All her grooming was done for her by her governess. Her father used to visit her every day. After she turned fifteen, he began to visit her once a week. And when she was sixteen, on seeing how her beauty had ripened, her father did not trust even him and stopped visiting her completely. But every week he would exchange letters with his daughter and the governess would keep the king informed about the girl's progress.

Before her eighteenth birthday, the king promised her that he would have a great party for her on the day of her birthday. Every eligible noble man from all over the kingdom and even the neighboring countries would be there and she would choose her husband from among them. The girl was very excited. Finally the day came around and the doors of the room were flung open and the young woman stepped out. She looked stunningly beautiful and everyone who saw her was moved to tears.

All that day she met her family and cousins and friends and everyone who saw her was filled with a mad joy compounded by a bitter sorrow because of her beauty. But the princess could not understand why people started to cry as soon as they saw her. She asked her governess why they were crying and the old woman brought her a mirror and when the princess saw her own beauty she began to cry too and went back to her room and stayed there all day, refusing to come out.

Finally her father asked her what the matter was and she said, Father, I will never find anyone as beautiful as I am. Men will love me for my good looks but what should I love them for? For their shallowness? Or for my own vanity? And the father was sad because he knew that she was right, she was a prisoner of her own beauty and his pride.

And he left her alone after that and did not bother her again. The princess lived the rest of her life in that room and although she was free to come and go as she pleased, she hardly ever left her room and met very few people. Still she was happy and many, many years after when she was old and her charms had faded a bit someone asked her if she regretted anything and she said that the only thing she regretted was that she never had a kitten when she was young. But now she had many cats."

"That's a sad story," said Karan, after a while, when Meera was silent.

"Not for the Princess because she was happy in the end," the girl replied

"Happiness is relative, I suppose," said Karan, "but joy, joy is special."

They sat in silence for a while.

"People around me would cry when I sang," said Meera. "For a while, when I was young, I was a singing sensation. But then I got tired of it. I felt like the Princess in the story. People loved me only for my singing. Nobody really loved me as a person."

"And now?" asked Karan

"I liked you from the moment I saw you first. But I thought you were in love with Stella."

Karan was quiet, thinking of what she had said. "I don't just like you, I love you," he said. "And you're wrong, when you sing people experience the emotions in your song, the emotions that you convey through your voice. That's why they loved you and will love you again."

"I don't want to be a star, Karan," said Meera. "I just want a family to love and be loved."

They were quiet while their food was served. Karan put his hand over hers and squeezed it. Silently they ate their food and when they were done they walked along the beach and bought ice candy from a vendor.

The sea breeze was cool and soothing and the couple held hands and walked, nibbling on their ice cream. When they were done, Karan called a rickshaw and rode with Meera back to her hostel. Before she left, she kissed him on the lips again, to the amazement and envy of the rickshaw driver.

Karan rode back to his apartment in a joyous daze. So many wonderful things in one day. Truly, this was the best day of his life so far.

Chapter Seventeen

The next day Mistry was at Karan's flat before his neighbor had even got out of bed. The stockbroker leaned on the calling bell till Karan stumbled out of bed and raced to the door, fumbling with the latch before flinging the door wide open.

"Mistry!" he exclaimed, seeing his friend standing there. "What are you doing here at this time of the morning?"

"We need to talk," said Mistry, walking past Karan into the flat. Karan followed him and sat opposite his friend. He was still in his night clothes, shorts and a night shirt and his hair was rumpled. There was stubble on his cheek and his teeth felt like they had a thick film of gum on them. Mistry on the other hand was smartly dressed in a well pressed formal shirt and trousers. He had shaved his cheeks to perfection and looked as fresh as a new born babe.

"What's the rush?" asked Karan. "Can't it wait till I have had my coffee and my shower?"

"No, it can't," said Mistry. "Have you picked more stocks yet?"

Karan got up and walked to his desk. Next to the PC was a sheet of paper which was filled with names. He handed it to Mistry.

"Here they are." he said "I sure hope you know what you are doing"

"I hope you do" said Mistry. "Did you hear your oracle's song when you picked these stocks?"

"Yes to your question," said Karan, "and no, I don't know what I am doing buying shares while listening to strange, music in my head."

"Never mind," said Mistry. "We're going to make a killing,"

He picked up his phone and got busy on it. After a while he was done. The broker put his phone away and got up.

"Enjoy your coffee and bath," said Mistry. "Tomorrow I'm going to present you with a fat check and then we're going to have a long talk and make some serious."

"What are we going to talk about?" said Karan, following Mistry to the door. "And what kind of plans?"

"I'll tell you tomorrow," said Mistry, turning at the door and bringing his fingertips to his forehead.

"Meanwhile, have a good day, guru," he said, saluting his friend with the tips of his fingers and a smile before he moved away to the elevator.

Karan closed the door and leaned against it. He thought for a while about the events of the previous day. Then he moved to his computer and inserted the CD he had recorded yesterday of Meera singing his songs. He put the volume up and closed his eyes and listened as her sweet voice transposed him to a distant place.

When the disc had played itself out, Karan opened his eyes and sat in reflection for a few minutes. This was it, he knew. This was the culmination of his life's work and hopes and dreams. Meera sang his songs with more feeling and emotive depth then even he had dreamed of when he wrote the music and wrung out the lyrics. He thought for a while on how he should proceed and then began to search the internet for names and numbers of recording studios. He was going to be famous. He was going to be appreciated. And he was going to get married.

The next day, Mistry came over with a check for five hundred thousand rupees. He handed it over to Karan whose eyes almost popped out of his head when he saw he figure.

"Don't sweat, Karan," said the stockbroker. "This is just a part of your earnings. You have at least four times that in stocks under your name."

Karan sat in a daze while his friend explained about how he had invested the money based on Karan's predictions. Finally, when Mistry came to the end of his longwinded speech, Karan realized that he had been asked a question.

"Huh?" said the musician

"Where have you been, buddy? Did you hear a word I just said?" asked Mistry.

"No, sorry, my mind was wandering," said Karan, trying to refocus on the conversation,

"I can see that," said his friend. He looked at Karan carefully.

"Something bothering you?" asked Mistry

"Meera was here last night," said Karan

Mistry stared at him "You dog! That was fast work!" he said admiringly.

"It's not what you think. She was here most of the day actually and just a small part of the night. By the way, has anyone ever told you that you have a dirty mind?"

"Frequently. Get on with your story," said Mistry.

"She was here to record some of my songs. And she has a truly amazing voice. I really think I am on to something here."

"Well, well," said Mistry. "So now you've got two things going. Your stock picking, oracle like abilities and your music which as you say might be a hit. Two pots on the stove. Life's looking up, eh! Good for you. I admire a person who believes in himself."

"You believe in yourself when you have no one else to believe in," said Karan "and I think I might be in love with her," he added

Mistry was aghast, "With whom?"

"Meera, of course, you ass. Whom did you think?"

Mistry composed himself and leaned forward, close to Karan. "Listen my friend," he started, speaking in a low, serious voice, searching for the right words.

"Love is a dangerous game. What you need is a nice homely wife who'll soon clear your mind of love and other stupid notions."

"You're a cynic, Mistry, you know that. That's your problem."

"No, that's not my problem, that's my saving grace. I may chase skirts but even I would never be stupid enough to fall in love with one of them."

Karan turned away and gazed out of the window. "You know, it's a real coincidence but Meera's old boyfriend happens to be Mansoor, the army guy who rescued me Stella and me during the earthquake."

Mistry stared at him, aghast again. "You mean that crazy guy who is running around with all those weapons, looking for someone to kill?"

"The same guy, but he wasn't crazy when she knew him."

"That's her naive opinion," said Mistry. "Listen, pal, we have a good thing going with these stocks that you picked. Don't throw it all away on some broad whom you think has a perfect voice and who's got a crazy boyfriend."

"Ex-boyfriend," corrected Karan, "and you're too late, Mistry" said Karan.

"You can't stop love. Just like you can't stop a runaway train. I am a lucky man"

"You may be a dead man soon," said Mistry, exasperated. "Listen, I'll tell you a story. It's true every word of it. Listen carefully.

There was this married guy, good job, fine children, pretty wife. He used to take his son to the park every evening and there he happened to meet this woman who had the habit of walking her dog every day at that particular time in the evening. It started innocently enough with casual conversation, a little light flirting and then it got more serious. Finally, it bloomed into a full blown affair.

The lady's husband was always travelling and this young father used to sneak into the woman's house every afternoon, after leaving the office early. But after a few months, the strain was too much for him and he wanted to end it. The woman wouldn't have it. She wanted him to leave his wife and marry her, after she divorced her husband. The man was stunned. He was only in it for the sex. He told her that there was no way that he was going to do that. The woman threw a fit. She threatened him that she would tell his wife everything. She didn't care if her husband came to know too but she knew for sure that the man's wife would leave him.

It so happened that the man was working for his father-in-law, who owned the business. He was in line to take over the company when the old man passed away. But he knew for sure that the old man would dump him if he came to hear about this affair. He was desperate. He did not know what to do. After speaking to a few of his friends, he decided that the only thing he would do was have her taken care of. By that, he meant, have her killed.

He got the name and number of a specialist hit man from a friend who had links with the local mafia. He contacted the hit man, and told him the whole story. The hit man listened carefully and after considering for a while he named his price. It was steep, but the man was more than willing to pay. He could easily get the money back when he was the owner of his father in law's company. He agreed and paid half the cash up front.

After a week, he didn't see or hear from his lover anymore. The hit man contacted him and told him that the job was done. He took the remainder of the cash and went to pay the hit man. The killer counted the money carefully and then turned his gun to the man.

"That lady I killed?" said the hit man. "You've been having an affair with my wife," the contract killer told him as he pulled the trigger. And that was the end of both the lovers."

Mistry sat back and regarded Karan who had been listening intently,

"And the moral of the story is..?" asked Karan.

"Never let your heart or any other body part, rule your head."

"Cynic," said Karan getting up and walking around. "You are a hard hearted cynic."

Mistry got up too and headed for the door,

"Well, don't say I didn't warn you," he said, shaking his head as he made for the door.

After he had left, Karan put the CD he had recorded last night with Meera into the player and with his eyes closed, listened to the music. Oh, perfect day! He thought to himself as the music flowed through the apartment.

Chapter Eighteen

Across the building, in the shade and shelter of the awnings of the shops, a badly dressed man watched the entrance of the apartment. He was tall and well built and if he had shaved and had a hair cut he could have pass off as a respectable young man. But now with his week old beard and dirty clothes, he was an object of fear and disgust. Pedestrians crossed the road to avoid walking close to him and though he tried to remain inconspicuous, he stood out like a blister on a thumb.

Mansoor was not worried. No one recognized him. For one thing no one came close enough to get a good look at him and secondly he looked nothing like the photo of the smart, clean cut officer which the papers had published. Mansoor was wearing a long overcoat, which itself was unusual given the growing heat of the day. What he did not know was the inquisitive waiter had phoned in his description to the police who now had an idea of what the renegade officer had looked like and how he was dressed.

Mansoor had seen Meera leave the apartment with Karan last night. He did not know what she had been doing there, but he knew she had been in Karan's fault all day yesterday. Mansoor had been at his post since the morning, after having followed Karan from the restaurant where he had eaten dinner with Meera on the previous occasion.

Last night, the couple had dinner together again and Mansoor was there, outside the restaurant, nibbling on piece of bread that he had scavenged from the streets. He had followed Karan back to the apartment after the musician had dropped Meera off at her hostel. Mansoor had been in another rick and watching closely. He knew what was happening between Karan and Meera. He knew why the man whose life he had saved was attracted to the young girl. The only thing he did not know was whether he would kill them both or kill only Karan. He had saved Karan's life and it now belonged to him. The girl had rejected him and now she was proving unfaithful.

Mansoor watched for a while longer and he guessed that Karan would not be leaning the apartment in the morning. Maybe now was the time to move in. He could go up to his flat and ring the bell and as soon as Karan opened the door he could kill him. Mansoor patted the gun sticking into the waistband of his trousers. The problem with the plan was that he would not be able to confront Meera. He wanted her to watch, at the very least. He decided he would not kill her but he would punish her. She would remember him. She would never forget him as long as she lived.

Last night he had slept on the beach and the rising moon had illuminated the sea for him. He had sat in the sand and gazed out at the waters, imagining their immense depth and breadth and the hidden power which lay beneath its calm exterior. He wished he had the power to command the waves, to order up another tsunami which this time would sweep through the whole city, razing everything in its path. And this time he would not be there to rescue the victims. Let them manage without him. He had sat and gazed at the moon and the sea and his mind slid further into the dark place, where no light ever shines.

In his flat, Karan began to make calls to people he knew in the music industry. First he scheduled a session at the recording studio and then he spoke to two of his acquaintances in the business. He convinced them to attend the recording session, telling them that he had new and revolutionary material that they would not want to miss hearing. Both the acquaintances, who worked for different labels knew that Karan understood music. They agreed to be there.

Next he called Mistry and told him that he wanted to sell all his stocks and put the money on one stock that he would pick. Karan decided that he would finance the production of his songs himself, if the recording company people did not want to take him up.

Mistry was surprised and tried to dissuade him, saying it was too risky to bet only on one stock. But Karan persuaded him. The songwriter had grown confident about his stock picking skills and he pointed out to the trader that he had not lost money yet, or made a wrong stock pick. Mistry reluctantly agreed to do as his friend wanted but he warned him again. Karan would not listen.

He was in love and nothing could go wrong.

After he had finished the phone calls, Karan ordered food and sat at his piano. He worked all day, composing new material and reworking older stuff. Outside Mansoor waited and watched, biding his time, like a jungle cat stalking his prey.

In her hostel, after work, Meera sang Karan's songs to herself as she sat and gazed out the window at the mango tree with its yellow leaves. Karan had called her and told her that the recording session was set for the next Saturday. He wanted to meet her on Wednesday to go over the music again and she had agreed, breaking her rule of not going out on a weekday. Now she found herself looking forward to her next meeting with Karan. She hugged herself and sang softly into the night.

Mansoor prowled the pavements all day. When the shopkeepers chased his him away from the area near their shops, he went to the beach, snarling and cursing like a whipped dog. He chose a spot from where he could watch the entrance of the apartment building. After a while, when the shopkeepers had retreated back to their shops and were busy he came out on the pavement again and paced up and down, ignoring the glares of the passer bys. He had decided that he would wait till Meera came back to Karan's apartment. Then he would catch both of them together and decide what he would do.

Mansoor had rescued five people during the earthquake and tsunami. One person died in a rescue attempt that could have gone either way. But in the fuss that followed the death of his subordinate, everyone had seemed to have forgotten about the five lives he had saved.

Karan's had been the first and what Mansoor had given him, now Mansoor would take back. His own career and life were ruined anyway. Apart from not being sufficiently grateful. Karan had the temerity to steal Mansoor's girlfriend. Now it was time he learnt his lesson.

Towards the middle of the day, Mansoor's stomach began to hurt him and he realized he had not eaten since the night before. He walked over to a vendor at the beach and bought the cheapest snacks that he could find. From a public tap he filled a discarded bottle with water.

Munching peanuts and sipping the water, he resumed his vigil, sitting on the sandy beach and staring at the gates of the apartment building. When the sun was past its zenith and his stomach no longer hurt him, Mansoor lay back, resting his head on the sand. He gazed at the blue sky where scattered puffs of clouds drifted gently past. There was a sea breeze blowing and he felt almost relaxed.

His mind drifted to his village in Gujarat where his old parents lived, along with his younger sister. They would be waiting for news of him, he knew. They probably hadn't heard anything about him since his last letter. His mother couldn't read and his father had trouble with his eyes. When his infrequent letters reached home, it was his sister who would read the letter out to his parents and they would question her about many little details.

Mansoor did not write often or very much about his own life and his letters were often terse. His little sister would embellish her brother's letter, filling in odd details which she guessed or imagined to be true.

After she had read the letter, Naina would sit and write to Mansoor telling him all the news of the village and how she longed to get away to the big city. She was finishing school next year and had dreams though how those dreams would be realized no one knew, least of all her. But she lived for her elder brother and trusted him to take care of her.

Mansoor closed his eyes and soon fell into a doze. He dreamt that he was returning to his village. There was a large group of people waiting to see him. When he reached the village, the people garlanded him with flowers and there was much cheering and rejoicing. He was taken to the center of the village where all the people had gathered around to hear him speak. There were even people from the neighboring town and camera crew from a national television channel.

Mansoor climbed up on the little podium they had built for him. He gazed down at the sea of faces turned up expectantly toward him. His parents and sister were sitting in the front row. Little children gazed at him with awe and young woman stared up at him with devout admiration. Mansoor looked at all these patient faces and the words would not come to his mouth. He looked up at the sky and saw dark clouds forming at the horizon. A flock of crows flew passed the sun, calling raucously.

Mansoor fumbled at the waist band of his pants and pulled out his two pistols. Pointing at the crowd he fired, again and again till the empty clicking of the hammer told him his bullets were spent and the fallen bodies of the people he loved told him that he would never disappoint them again.

When he woke, the sun had started its descent and the air was cooler. Mansoor pulled his coat around him, shivering a little, both from the memory of his dream and from the cool air. He had not taken his coat off even in the heat of the day because of the weapons that he was carrying. He had two pistols tucked securely into his pants and three hand grenades which were clipped on to the inside of the coat. He meant to use the grenades first and keep the pistols for the end. He turned and gazed at the infinite horizon, where sky met sea and something he saw in his mind made his mouth drop open in wonder and desire. He blinked several times and turned and headed for the apartment. As the night began to fall, he resumed his pacing of the streets, often glancing up at the flat where Karan lived, wondering if today would be the day he would get his vengeance.

Chapter Nineteen

Karan switched on the lights in his apartment. Night had fallen, almost before he knew it. He was satisfied with his day's work. Sitting at the piano all day he had prepared six songs more for Meera to record. That would make a total of eighteen songs to be recorded on Saturday and then he would have to push the recording companies to have faith in his work. His and Meera's, he reminded himself.

With a satisfied sigh, he sank back into his armchair and considered how his life had changed so rapidly in the last two weeks. Just before the tsunami, he was broke and struggling and just as the storm had wrecked havoc, so too it had changed his fortunes but for the better.

Briefly he wondered about Stella but already her face was fading in his memory. What she had told him about the gift for prophecy still remained in his mind because he had the evidence of his considerably enriched bank account. Karan then remembered what he had told Mistry. He wanted to put all his earnings on a single stock, a stock that he would pick and would rise so rapidly and so dramatically that it would make him richer than his wildest dreams. That is, richer than the dreams he had before the tsunami but now his dreams were a whole lot bigger. With the money that he earned he would launch his musical career.

Karan went over to the computer and opened the list of traded companies. He ran his finger over the names which were now familiar to him till he stopped at one which seemed to jump out at him. It was a company called Peerless Infrastructure. This seemed like a good bet to Karan. The country sorely needed massive development in infrastructure. Roads and rail bridges would sprout everywhere. It seemed like a good bet to him.

Grabbing a pen from his desk he jotted down the company's name and then called Mistry on the phone. With the phone balanced on his shoulder, he waited for his friend to pick up and only then did he realize that he had not heard the oracle's tune when he had picked the stock. Karan hung up the phone before Mistry could pick up and thought hard. He tried to recall the tune in his head and pictured the stock in his head. He was not sure anymore if that was the way to do it.

Previously, when he had picked the stocks, he would wait for the song to start in his head before he stopped at a name. Now it was the other way around. Did it make a difference? Karan wasn't sure.

Just then the phone rang. Karan looked at the number on the screen and realized it was Mistry returning his call. He had to trust his intuition. He answered the phone

"Hi, Mistry," Karan spoke into the phone. "Yes, I had called you. Can you tell me what the total value of all my stock holdings is right now? Yes' I'll wait."

He head on to the phone, repeating the name Peerless, Peerless in his mind.

Mistry spoke into the phone.

"Twenty three hundred thousand rupees?" repeated Karan, his heart jumping. "Listen, I want you to sell everything and buy shares in a company called Peerless Infrastructure. The share price is quite low at the moment. No, I am sure. Just listen."

Karan stopped talking and listened while his friend tried to convince him about the dangers of putting all his eggs in one basket.

"I'm going to go for it, Mistry." said Karan finally, when the stock broker had stopped talking. As soon as he said the words he heard the mystic tune start up in his head. His voice became firmer.

"Please. Just do this for me." Karan held on to the phone a little longer while Mistry pleaded with him and then he put the phone down.

Mistry had promised to do as he wanted first thing tomorrow morning. Karan went to the window and looked out. He started to whistle. Through the window he could see the streets down below. There were people moving about, some shopping some hurrying on their way home. His eye caught sight of a solitary figure standing on the road across the apartment. The man was wearing a long overcoat.

As Karan watched the man, wondering why he was dressed in a coat in this warm weather, he heard the tune start up in his head. He was surprised, having no idea what it meant. The figure looked strangely familiar but it could not be anyone he knew. As Karan watched the stranger looked up directly and it seemed to Karan that their eyes met, although he was too far away to see the other man's eyes. Now the tune in his head was deafening and Karan had to put his hand up to rub at his forehead. The stranger was still staring at him and the music in Karan's head swelled to a shattering crescendo. Karan cried out and stumbled away from the window. He fell to the ground but managed to break his fall by grabbing on to the table which was nearby. The music had stopped.

Karan slowly scrambled to his feet wondering what had just happened. He decided to go and have a long shower. Truing to the window, he glanced down again but the stranger in the overcoat was nowhere to be seen. Karan shrugged and moved away. The stress and excitement of the last few days, he told himself. He stripped of f his clothes and got into the shower and let the water wash his troubles away.

At his office, Mistry put down the phone after his conversation with Karan. For the first time since he had taken to investing in stocks recommended by his naive friend, he was disturbed. Although he had never questioned the rationale behind Karan's choice, he had always been careful, first investing small sums and always spreading the investment over several stocks. Of course, not a single stock that Karan had picked had failed so far. Still, the thought of betting all his now considerable earnings on a single stock gave Mistry the jitters. He decided that he would stay out of it, but he would do as Karan wanted.

Turning to his desktop computer, Mistry called up Karan's file and checked the investments under his friend's name. His net worth on stocks was a little above 2.3 million rupees. Peerless was trading at about 200 rupees a share so Karan would be able to purchase a considerable sum. But Mistry knew that, apart from the risk of putting all his money on one stock, Infrastructure was a risky business. Companies would lose contacts or take huge loans to complete existing ones. The only thing that gave Mistry a slight hope was that Karan had an impeccable record. Shaking his head at the improbability of the situation, Mistry made out the buy order.

With a few clicks of the mouse it was accomplished. The trade was now irrevocable. Either Karan would lose all his money or he would make a lot of it. Mistry was staying out of it and he hoped for his friend's sake that his oracle had not deserted him.

Pushing away from his desk, Mistry got up and stretched. It had been a long day and it was time to go home now. He switched off the lights and locked the door to the office and rode the elevator down. As he walked to his car which was parked in the office lot, he began to hum a little song to himself. It was something that he had heard Karan play on the piano. Quite catchy, he thought. Mistry got into his car and drove away, planning to stop at a bar and have a drink or two before he got home.

Chapter Twenty

Mansoor was watching the apartment when he saw Mistry's car drive up. It was late, close to midnight. The ex-soldier watched as the stocky stockbroker got out of the car and walked a little unsteadily to the building. Maybe it was time to do some reconnaissance, thought Mansoor, checking to see where the watchman was, He walked along the pavement till he found a suitable spot. Climbing up a signpost, he jumped over the wall.

Mistry had just entered the building and Mansoor hurried to catch up. He ran across the foyer. The watchman was busy closing the gates to the apartment complex. At the elevator, Mansoor came upon Misty who was holding his brief case and humming a little tune, waiting for the lift to arrive. Misty glance at Mansoor and shrank back a little. Mansoor looked dangerous and Mistry was alarmed. Just then the elevator announced its arrival with a muted chime. The doors glided open.

Mistry quickly stepped in and pressed the button for the door to close but Mansoor was quick and got in just before the doors shut. Mistry moved back against the wall of the lift while Mansoor glared at him. The indicator sign flashed the floor numbers and when they came to Mistry's floor, the stockbroker hurriedly got out of the apartment. Mansoor watched him go. The same floor as Karan, he thought. Probably his neighbor and friend too. Mansoor pressed the button for the lobby. When he reached the bottom, he moved quietly to the wall and jumped over again.

When Mistry got out of the lift he couldn't stop shaking. There had been something very threatening and ominous about that man in the lift. Misty fumbled for his keys and then he saw the light under the door of Karan's fault. Moving to his neighbor's door, he leaned on the bell. Karan soon appeared.

"Mistry!" exclaimed Karan "What's happened? You look like you've seen a ghost."

"I saw something a lot worse," said Mistry, stumbling in past his friend. "There was this evil looking man in the lift with me and I was sure that he was going to attack me."

"What evil looking man? And why would he attack you?"

"He was wearing a dirty overcoat and I just got this feeling that he hated my guts. I wasn't scared that he would rob me, it wasn't that. I was sure he would kill me if he could."

"Which floor was he going to?"

"I don't know," said Mistry "He did not press any of the buttons which was strange in itself."

"He's probably a visitor staying temporarily I one of the flats above us."

"What struck me was the greasy overcoat he was wearing." Misty had recovered somewhat now. He sat down on Karan's armchair.

"Have you ever seen someone wearing an overcoat in this city?"

"No, well, wait a moment. Yes actually I did, this evening. And he may have been the same person that you saw. When I looked out my window I saw a guy in an overcoat looking up at the building. He seemed to be looking directly at this flat." said Karan.

"It's the same guy" Mistry shouted, all excited again. "He's the one! Quick call the cops"

"Hold on, hold on," said Karan, raising his hands in front of Mistry.

"Calm down. What are we going to tell the police? Its no crime to hang around on the road or ride in a lift.. For now, what we can do is call the security and ask if this guy is staying in the building"

Karan picked up the intercom and connected to the security. He spoke briefly into the phone and then out the instrument down.

"He says that you are the only person who entered the building in the last 30 minutes"

"So who was that guy I rode with, a ghost?" said Mistry, nervously.

"Relax," said Karan, holding out his hands again. "I saw him too, remember. Tomorrow we'll check if he's still there and if he is, we'll find out who he is and what he's doing here."

"Yes," said Mistry, subduing again, "we'll do that tomorrow. Meanwhile tonight don't forget to lock up tight. I suggest you close your windows too. He could get in that way."

Mistry got up to leave.

Karan laughed, "I don't think so. But I will be careful and you be too."

He walked his friend to the door and wished him goodnight. When Mistry had entered his own apartment, Karan locked the door and then went to peer out the window. The street below was deserted and after a while Karan drew the curtains, switched off the light and went to bed.

Mansoor was on the beach, lying on the sand and staring up at the golden orb of the moon. The police had been here a while ago, chasing vagrants like himself from the beach and Mansoor had hidden behind a street vendor's stall till they had left. They wouldn't be back tonight, he knew. Now he had the beach to himself as the other homeless people had moved on. Mansoor glanced away from the moon at another part of the night sky and saw a brilliant star. It was larger than the other stars nearby and was easily the brightest light in the night sky after the moon.

Mansoor kept gazing at the star. His eyes grew heavy and it seemed to him that the light was getting brighter and brighter. Suddenly a shadow crossed the light and he realized that there was someone standing in the starlight. Mansoor opened his eyes wide in shock and surprise. It was a young woman, dressed in a flowing white robe, her hair cascading over her shoulders. The girl's face was glowing, as if illuminated from within, and there was something familiar about her.

At first Mansoor thought it was his sister and then realized it was not. It was someone he had seen but did not know.

"Mansoor," the woman called, softly but urgently.

Her voice was low and lilting. Mansoor started and stood up. He was very frightened now.

"Mansoor," the girl called again. Her voice was insistent and this time he replied "Yes," he said stammering

"Do you know who I am?" Recognition flooded his mind. This was the girl whose body he had pulled out of the building, when he had rescued Karan. Her name was Stella.

"You're dead" said Mansoor, shrinking back.

"You don't really understand what that means, Mansoor" the girl spoke softly. "I had simply gone away to another place but now I am back."

Mansoor was terrified. He looked up and down the beach but there was no one else in sight.

"Mansoor," Stella called again.

"Yes," he whined "What do you want from me?"

"You know what I want you to do," said the apparition.

"Yes," said Mansoor, cringing. He knew only too well.

"Please do it," said Stella

"I will," Mansoor moaned. It was all he could manage.

"I'll be waiting and watching Mansoor," said Stella. "And I'll be back"

As Mansoor gazed in terror, she faded slowly and after a while all he could see was the bright light of the star, which was far, far away.

Mansoor wiped the sweat from his brow. The sea breeze was blowing strong now and he felt a sudden chill. He was scared. He knew what she wanted him to do. Somehow, he knew. But he didn't know if he could do it. He stared at the moon and back to the star again.

"Take me with you" he whispered, forlornly, wishing he could live forever in the warm glow of the light he had just seen.

In her bed, Meera tossed and turned. "Stella," she whispered and suddenly she was wide awake. She sat up in bed and though the window she could see the light of a distant star. Stella she whispered again and then she added a prayer.

In his flat, Karan too woke. Something had crossed his mind in a dream but he could not remember what it was. He heard the mysterious tune in his head and he lay back, his head against the pillow. He wondered what it all meant.

Mistry woke at the same time and got out of bed. He stood scratching his head, wondering what had woken him. Then he decided to walk to the fridge to get a drink of water. On his way back he checked his computer. Logging into Karan's trading account he checked the last order he had placed for his friend

"Executed," the screen flashed.

On the beach, Mansoor had fallen into a dreamless sleep. Night birds flew silently past the moon and the star shone down its eternal light.

Chapter Twenty One

The next morning Mistry was at Karan's flat early.

"I couldn't sleep," he explained apologetically to a sleepy eyed Karan.

"Let's check from your window if the guy is still there"

They walked to the window and looked out but they could see no sign of the stranger in the overcoat.

"He's gone" said Karan. "Don't worry, I'll keep checking all day to see if he comes back and if he does I'll call you. We can go together and talk to him."

"Okay," shrugged Mistry.

"Did you put my money in the Peerless Stock?" asked Karan

"I've placed the order," said Mistry. "I sure hope you know what you are doing" he said fervently. "Putting all your money on one stock is a dangerous business."

"I told you, I have no idea what I am doing when it comes to stocks."

Mistry shook his head in dismay

"Well, you're going alone on this one. I am selling all the stocks that you picked but I'm not investing in this one"

"Lost faith in my fortune telling?" teased Karan

"I may be stupid but I'm not that stupid. Luck needs a bit of effort to be effective."

"If it did, they wouldn't call it luck. Besides, it's not luck, remember. I am supposed to be able to see the future."

"It's your decision" said Mistry "now if you'll excuse me I have to go and get ready for work. Call me if the vagrant reappears."

"Will do," said Karan, closing the door behind his friend.

After Mistry had left, Karan prepared breakfast. After he had eaten, he set about to clean the flat. He didn't have a maid to do his housework for him as he couldn't afford one before. Now he had the money but since he was used to doing the daily chores he felt he could manage without any help. If he was married on the other hand, Meera could help him. Or she could get a maid if she wanted. Karan stopped what he was doing, surprised by his own thoughts. He was actually imagining married life with Meera. Did he really want to marry her?

He considered the question and decided, yes, he did. He walked over to an armchair and sat on it thinking. He knew he was in love with her, but somehow he had never considered marrying her. Now he had to ask himself if he was prepared to spend the rest of his life with this girl? And even if he was, would she agree to marry him?

Karan was not a successful musician. Every effort he had made to have his songs recorded and released by a recording label had failed. But he knew enough of music to know that Meera had great potential to become a genuinely successful singer. And if she wasn't singing his material, she could sing someone else's songs. He needed her more than she needed him. Karan decided that the right thing to do was to wait till the sings were released and see what kind of an effect success had on the young girl. He was quite certain that one of the two recording company executives would be able to see the potential in the music and sign both Karan and Meera on to their label. Once the album came out, it would be Meera as the singer who would get all the attention. She would have a lot of fans and admirers then and things might change.

Slowly Karan got up from the chair and picked up his duster. He resumed his cleaning, feeling a little despondent. He had waited so long, he could wait a just a little longer, he reasoned with himself.

In the restaurant where Karan and Meera had met twice lunch, the romantic waiter was thinking about them. Joseph was an incurable romantic. There were several other regular couples at the restaurant and he and his wife knew a lot more about them then they would ever have dreamed possible.

Joseph was an adept lip reader in two languages, from years of observation and practice. What he could not lip read or overhear, he could fill in using a little bit of his imagination. His wife waited eagerly for the updates on the lives of the various couples that frequented the little restaurant. Of course, the happy culmination of each story was when the couple finally got married, after which Joseph and his wife lost interest in them. It also happened that sometimes the couple would have a fight and break up. Then one of two things happened. Either they would patch up in a few days or the boy and girl would arrive alone and separately at the restaurant, sit and eat or drink alone, staring sadly into space, and then leave. Sometimes one or the other of them would turn up with a new partner.

These were the intrigues of daily life in the restaurant. Joseph loved his job and the opportunity it gave him to witness real life love stories. One day, when he was retired, he would write a screenplay, he sometimes thought. It would make a great TV reality show.

These days Joseph often thought of Meera. Sometimes his wife would ask him about her. But since that last visit with her new boyfriend he hadn't seen her. Joseph approved of the new boyfriend. He seemed to be a mild mannered, gentle man, more suited to Meera's personality than her previous boyfriend who had been a macho lout. Joseph had witnessed their break up, when Meera had told the lout that she did not want to see him anymore. He felt like cheering when he heard her say that, knowing it took no small amount of courage on her part to stand up to her boyfriend who was a big man. He wasn't probably a bad man either, thought the waiter, trying to be fair, but she just wasn't his type. And she had split up with him in just in time. Joseph knew that Mansoor was wanted by the police and that's why when he saw someone whom he thought looked like the renegade office man stalking Meera he had called the police.

Actually he had called a friend who was a policeman. His friend had told him to call if he saw Mansoor again. Joseph had described how Mansoor was dressed and the policeman had written down the description and assured him that he would inform the Army.

Once Meera had come to the restaurant a long time ago with another girl whom Joseph at first took to be her sister. The girls were alike, short and small made with tumbling hair up to their shoulders. They both spoke in the same way, with low, lilting voices. Then he had heard Meera call her companion Stella and he knew they were not related. Joseph often wondered about Stella, he had not seen her since that day. Maybe she had married and moved away. Somehow, the romantic dreamer had the feeling that Stella was happy woman now.

Just as he was thinking about Meera and Stella, the door of the restaurant opened and Meera walked in alone. Joseph's eyes almost popped out of his head. Dream of an angel and hear the flutter of wings, he told himself as he hurried to meet her. She returned his gracious smile, knowing him well by sight. Joseph led her to a table in the corner, assuming that her boyfriend would come to meet her but she told him she wanted to sit near the glass front window at the other end of the restaurant. Joseph held her chair out for her and then took her order of iced latte. He smiled at her again as he hurried off to bring her order.

Meera looked around the restaurant. There were two other couples there and they were engrossed in each other. She wished that Karan was here. She had left the call center at lunchtime because she felt she wanted to be alone for a while. She normally ate at the canteen with her colleagues. Today she wanted to avoid the incessant chatter of her companions.

As she was sitting there, thinking of Karan and their songs, her phone rang. She reached for it excitedly, hoping it was him but when she saw the number on the screen she realized that it wasn't.

"Hello," she spoke into the phone, wondering who it was calling her.

"Meera," said a familiar voice on the other side and her heart sank. Not again. Not now.

"Mansoor," she spoke softly but Joseph approaching her table with the latte overheard her. He placed the latte in front of her and withdrew to a discreet distance, staying within hearing. He could see that she was troubled.

"My Meera," Mansoor said. "Why are you not faithful to me?"

"Mansoor, listen to me," said Meera urgently. "You need help. Give yourself up and we will take care of you. I promise. Don't do anything stupid."

Mansoor laughed. "Are you worried about me now?" he jeered. "You should worry about your boyfriend. He's the one in danger."

"Mansoor," Meera spoke quickly. "Where are you calling from?"

"I'm calling from a payphone," said Mansoor. "I just wanted to let you know that I know what you are up to. I saved your boyfriends life and he repaid me by stealing you from me. Now I'll take back what I gave him."

"Mansoor, no," Meera was crying now and Joseph's heart broke. The swine, he thought.

Mansoor hung up the phone, having heard Meera sobbing. There will be more tears to come, he thought to himself, satisfied.

Meera put the phone down and wiped her eyes. She drank half her latte and left what was remaining. Putting some money down on the table, she fled the restaurant, not meeting the waiter's eyes.

Joseph watched her go sadly, shaking his head. Some men should be strung up by their toes for the way they treat women, he thought. He cleared Meera's table and then went to the back of the restaurant and called his friend, the policeman.

"Yes, I'm sure," Joseph said on the phone. "And I believe he was threatening her. Look, I want you to do something for me. Have a policeman follow her around for a few days. Listen, you can arrange it. If you catch him you'll get all the credit. And you will catch him,"

Joseph listened to his friend on the other end of the line and then put the pone down. He felt better about Meera now. There would be someone watching over her.

After a while, he called his wife and told her the news. His wife praised him for his quick action and worried about Meera.

"She'll be fine," said Joseph confidently. "This romance will have a happy ending."

"I hope so," his wife sighed. "I can't help thinking about that poor man. He must be suffering so."

"Who are you talking about?" asked Joseph, puzzled,

"Mansoor, her old boyfriend. I know he has a mother somewhere who is worried sick about him."

"Oh, him," said Joseph. Sometimes he wondered about his wife. Didn't she know that even a love story had to have a villain? You weren't supposed to feel sorry for the bad guy.

"Well, got to get back to work," said Joseph

He put down the phone and went to his stations by the window ignoring customers at several tables who were trying to attract his attention. I hope she's okay, he thought. I hope nothing bad happens to her.

Chapter Twenty Two

Meera ran from the restaurant, tears flowing down her cheeks. Once she had known Mansoor, and she had thought she known him well. But now he was someone else and the person she had known had disappeared. She stopped and wiped her eyes and fumbled in her handbag for her phone. She had to warn Karan. He would know what to do.

She dialed Karan's number and was relieved when he answered quickly. "Meera," he said. "a nice surprise. I was just thinking of you."

"Karan," she sobbed into the phone and Karan was instantly concerned. "What happened?" he asked

"Mansoor called me," said Meera trying to keep her voice from breaking. "He has gone mad. He said he's going to kill you." She sobbed into the phone.

There was a pause while Karan digested what she had just said.

"Did he say why he wants to kill me?" he asked after a while.

"He said he gave you your life and you repaid him by stealing me from him. Now he wants his revenge."

"I thought the two of you had broken up."

"That's what I told him," said Meera, "but he can't seem to accept it. Oh, Karan, I'm so scared."

"Listen, don't worry," said Karan, thinking hard. He remembered Mistry's encounter with the stranger on the lift.

"I don't remember him very clearly," said Karan. "Can you describe what he looks like?"

"He's tall and well built, looks very fit." said Meera. "And he's got a full beard and dark, penetrating eyes. When he looks at you it seems like he's looking right through you."

"Wait," said Karan, "I saw someone hanging about outside the apartment yesterday. I couldn't see his eyes but he was tall and had a beard. And the same man rode up the elevator with Mistry late last night. Mistry was terrified. He said the man looked extremely dangerous."

"It's him, it's him," said Meera in a panic. "Karan, I'm coming there. I want to talk to him before he does something really stupid."

"That could be dangerous, Meera," said Karan slowly. "Shouldn't we call the police He's a wanted man."

"Just let me talk to him first," pleaded Meera. "The police will hurt him. He's not really a bad man. He has a mother and a sister."

"Are you really sure that you want to talk to a man who is armed and dangerous and a little crazy as well?"

"Yes," said Meera.

There is a power in innocence which makes anything seem possible, thought Karan. And there is a cynic in experience who has experienced the futility of hope.

Karan walked over to the window and peered outside. There was no sign of the man in the overcoat.

"Well, come on over and we'll see if we can find him. He's not here today."

"Thanks, Karan." said Meera sincerely. "I have to go back to the office and tell them that I need to leave early.

Then I'll head over to your flat. I should be there in about two hours. Promise me that you won't call the police if you see him."

"I promise," said Karan, shaking his head, knowing that he shouldn't agree.

"Thanks again. See you soon," Now her voice had perked up. Meera put the phone away and looked around to find an auto rickshaw.

The policeman who was watching her spoke into his radio.

Karan put the phone down and went over to peer out the window again. Still no sign of Mansoor. If it was him. He decided to call Mistry.

When Mistry answered the phone, Karan told him about Meera's call.

"This is getting interesting," said Mistry. "Listen, I don't have a whole lot of work to do today. I'm coming over. Let us go and talk to the watchman and some of the shopkeepers. They would have been sure to have noticed a big man in an overcoat."

"I was hoping you would say that," said Karan. "We'll wait till Meera get here and then we can all go together."

"Right," said Mistry, sounding much more confident than the previous night. "See you soon."

Karan looked around the flat, checking that it wasn't too much of a mess. He would soon be seeing Meera. He noted the time. Maybe he should prepare lunch. They could all eat together and then in the evening after they had resolved the issue of Mansoor, Mistry would leave and he and his girl could have dinner alone and together. The day looked promising.

Then he had another thought and frowned. If they did find Mansoor, what were they to do? Should he allow Meera to talk to him? Not without his being present, that was for sure. Karan still did not like the idea of not calling the police but he had realized that Meera was very upset about what had happened to Mansoor. He was after all, someone that she knew once. And he did save Karan's life, even if he had only been doing his job. Karan shrugged. He would play it by ear. Just one step at a time.

A while alter the door bell rang and Karan jumped up to answer it. There stood Mistry holding a packet of food in one hand and a tub of ice cream in the other.

"I thought we should eat first before embarking on our dangerous and noble quest" he said.

"That's right," said Karan. No mission should be carried out on an empty stomach. He took the parcels from Mistry and put them in the kitchen. Mistry followed him there.

The door bell rang.

This time Karan ran to the door, leaping over the sofa which was in the way. He opened it, big smile on his face and there stood Meera, holding a packet of food in one hand and a tub of ice cream in the other.

"I thought you wouldn't have eaten yet," said Meera, smiling at him.

"More food," said Karan, bemused. "Come in, come in."

He held the door open for her and Meera walked in. She saw Mistry and stopped. "Meera, you remember Mistry, my friend and neighbor," said Karan.

"Yes" said Meera, putting the food down and holding out her hand. Mistry covered her small hand with his two meaty paws, clasping it warmly.

"Very pleased to see you again," he said, beaming down at the petite girl.

****

Below the surface of the earth, there was more movement. A contra flow of molten mass caused the movement of the plates to dampen. The next earthquake had been avoided.

On the surface of the earth, over the massive ocean, air masses flowed and converged. There was a huge storm brewing. And it was headed towards land.

****

Chapter Twenty Three

Meera helped Karan lay the table and heat up the food. While they were eating, Mistry told Karan that he had bought the shares in Peerless in Karan's name. Now Karan's portfolio consisted only of Peerless stock.

"Not much movement in the market today," said Mistry. "The shares were trading slightly lower after the purchase."

"What was the initial price?" asked Karan.

"About 1000 rupees a share which I think is overpriced for the stock. But now you own 2300 shares in the stock and its current value is a little less than 2.3 million rupees. And I have to tell you again that I don't think this was a good decision." said Mistry

"Well, none of the stocks that we bought together were rational decisions. I take it that you haven't invested any of your money in Peerless?" asked Karan

"No," said Mistry. "I've also sold o all the other stocks that you recommended. I've made a very nice profit but I think your luck is due to change for the worse."

"It's not luck, its prophecy," said Karan, laughing.

"Don't laugh," chided Mistry. "Money is never something to laugh about."

Meera was following the conversation and now she spoke up

"Is this what you were telling me about your foresight which you think Stella has give you?" she asked

"Yes," said Karan "I've been picking stocks at random and my selections have all done well."

"Does it work only on stocks or on other things too?"

"So far only on stocks. But it may be as Mistry said that I've just been lucky. I don't know really, it is too confusing. But I do know that she gave me the confidence to believe in myself. Which is not so difficult really, when you have no one else to believe in."

"Anyone can pick a few winners," said Mistry," given enough time and a bit of luck. They usually start to think that they can never lose and end up making some bad choices. The trick is to know when to quit."

Meera didn't say anything but she looked thoughtful. They finished their meal and cleared up, deciding to save the ice cream for later. All three of them were now thinking about Mansoor and Mistry was the first one to bring up his name.

"I wonder why Mansoor stalked me that night. Why would he have a grudge against me and how does he even know that I know you?" he asked, looking worried.

"Maybe he doesn't," said Karan. "You just happened to be there at the same time that he got into the building."

"I don't believe in coincidences anymore," grumbled Mistry.

"If he's been watching the building for a few days he might have seen the two of you together," said Meera.

"That's possible," replied Karan, getting up from his chair, "and now let us head down. We'll talk to the watchman first."

The three of them rode the elevator to the ground floor and walked up to the security post at the gates of the building. The two watchmen, seeing them approaching, stood up in anticipation.

Mistry spoke first.

"Last night when I was in the lift there was another man, tall, bearded and wearing a long dirty overcoat. Do you have any idea who he was?"

The security guards looked at each other and shrugged."

There's no one who looks like that staying here," said one of them, a youngish man, thin with a prominent nose that gave him the appearance of a hawk.

"We were on duty last night" said the other, a short fat man with a large stomach, who had the asymmetrical features of a comic actor in a movie. "Till midnight. We saw you come in" he continued, indicating Mistry, "but no one else came in at that time."

"Well, I didn't imagine him," said Mistry, a little annoyed. "Don't you people patrol the area around the building? He must have jumped over the wall or he could have been hiding inside the compound all evening."

The security guards looked at each other but didn't reply. Then the hawk faced one spoke. "Even if he had jumped over the wall we would have seen him when he entered the building because then we can see the entrance from our post."

"That why he entered the building at the same time as me," said Mistry. "You may have seen a figure entering and thought it was me. You didn't realize that two people had entered."

The guards looked at each other guiltily. "Sorry, boss" said the fat one.

"Okay, there's nothing we can do about that now. But please be alert. Nothing happened this time but next time we, and you, might not be so lucky"

"What we want to ask you, "said Karan, "is have you seen a tall bearded man in an overcoat hanging about the street in the last few days?"

The guards looked at each other and suddenly the fat one spoke up excitedly,

"Yes, we have. A few days ago one of the shopkeepers was having an argument with a man who looks like you described. Apparently this stranger had been lurking about outside his shop and the owner was complaining that he was scaring away customers. He asked him to move on and the two of them had a loud shouting match. That was what drew our attention. We went out on the road to see what all the fuss was about."

"What happened then?" asked Karan, "Where did he go?"

"He walked on towards the beach. At first he was not going to move from where he was but then other shop owners came out of their shops and together they threatened the man. At first I thought he was going to take on all of them together. He certainly seems capable of it and even the shopkeepers were a little nervous. But finally he turned away and moved on towards the beach."

"Did you see him again after that?" asked Meera

"No," said the guard, "but it's not likely that he would come back because they warned him that they would call the police if he turned up here again. Are you sure that it was the same man who was in the elevator last night?

"We think so," said Mistry, "unless there are two people in the neighborhood crazy enough to wear an overcoat in this weather."

"We thought he was a flasher," said the watchmen, and the other laughed, glancing at Meera. He caught Karan's eye and looked away hurriedly.

From the guard post they could see a small area of the beach. Karan pointed it out to the others.

"That's where he could have been watching the building from" he said. "And that's where he probably was when he saw you come in. There are a number of places where he could have got over the wall."

"True," said Mistry "Let us go over to the beach and talk to the vendors there. They might know something,"

Before leaving Mistry admonished the watchmen again and then the three of them walked through the gate and headed to the beach. They walked shoulder to shoulder, with Meera in the middle and Karan and Mistry on either side. The two men towered above her and Meera felt a strong sense of security walking between these two friends. She also felt happy and slipped her hand into Karan's who looked at her in surprise and then clasped her hand firmly and eagerly. They reached the beach and looked up and down. There was the usual crowd on the beach, sight seers, people strolling, couples walking hand in hand and the hawkers. There was no sign of anyone wearing an overcoat.

"Do you really think he's going to be here?" asked Mistry.

"I think he sleeps on the beach. It would be the easiest place for him to hide. Many vagrants sleep here at night and move on in the day, scrounging for food. There are police patrols who come around supposedly to clear any late night stragglers from the beach but they invariably come at fixed times and the vagrants know how to avoid them. Our best chance is to talk to some of the hawkers. They come here every day and they would quickly spot any new faces."

The three friends began to walk along the beach. Meera looked out at the ocean. Waves crashed into the shore and the wind was strong.

"There's a storm coming," she said.

"Oh really?" said Mistry looking around, "did you read the signs in the weather?"

"Actually, I read it in the paper," said Meera, laughing. "There's a cyclone forming in the Bay of Bengal and it is expected to hit the coast tomorrow evening."

"That means we'll get a lot of rain and strong winds. The beach will be deserted then. Even the homeless people will not stay here in a storm."

"So if Mansoor is sleeping here every night, where would he go tomorrow?" asked Meera.

"Maybe he'll want to move on tomorrow. Remember, he knows the police and the army are after him so he would be keen to leave the city."

"After he finishes what he came here to do," said Karan

"Which is, to kill you," said Mistry

"So you're saying that he might make his move tomorrow?" asked Karan.

"It's possible," said Meera. "He's been in town and on the run for several days."

"Why hasn't he done it before?" asked Karan

"I think he wanted Meera here. He might have guessed that once he had called her she would come to you," said

Mistry. "He'll want her to appreciate what he's doing for her," said the stockbroker.

"For me?" exclaimed Meera. "He's doing this for me?"

"Of course" said Karan. "He wants to win you back and he thinks this is best the way of doing it."

Meera thought about this for a minute "So supposing he sees that we've had a fight and broken up and suppose I stay away from you, do you think that would make him change his mind about what he wants to do?"

"I don't think so," said Mistry. "He's probably dead set in doing this. And I have a feeling," Mistry glanced up at the black clouds accumulating in the sky "that he's going to do it very quickly."

They had reached the stalls of one of the hawkers, a man Karan knew by sight and whom he sometimes bought his lemonade from.

"Hello, brother" said Karan. He made a little small talk with the man and then he asked, "have you by any chance seen a tall, bearded man in along overcoat hanging around on the beach?"

The vendor wanted to know what an overcoat was and Karan described it to him. He thought for a while and finally spoke

"I saw a man dressed that way a few days ago but I have not seen him after that," said the hawker.

"Do you think that man is seeping on the beach at night?"

"It's possible, but I haven't seen him here in the mornings when I set up my stall. And I'm usually here quite early when some of the other bums are still sleeping on the sand," said the salesman.

Karan thanked him and the three companions moved on. They stopped and asked two more hawkers. One of them said he had seen the man in the overcoat a few days ago but not after that. The other hawker had noticed the man at all.

They continued to walk on deciding not to enquire any more. They kept their eyes open, noting the people who passed by and studying the places where someone might hide. There were a few open air restaurants scattered on the beach and one area where a cluster of trees grew.

"He could be sleeping in there at night," said Mistry, indicating the trees.

"Have you wondered why he wears that overcoat all the time?" asked Meera. "He would know that he stands out wearing such clothing."

"He wears it so that he can hide the weapons he's carrying," said Karan

"That's not it," said Meera. "He could still hide a gun if he was wearing normal clothes. He's wearing an overcoat because, once he takes it off, he becomes invisible."

Karan and Mistry stopped and turned to look at her.

"Don't you see?" said Meera, holding out her hands, palms up. "Everyone's looking for a man wearing an overcoat so if he's not wearing one, nobody would look at him twice."

"Yes, it's true," said Karan slowly. "A perfect disguise. Hiding in plain sight."

"So when he wants to be noticed he wears the overcoat and struts around, maybe even creating a scene when he can," said Mistry, "and when he doesn't want to be seen, he just takes the coat off and maybe has a shave and haircut and walks around invisible."

"That's it," said Karan. "After he rode the elevator with you he has changed his appearance. That's why no one has noticed him around recently."

"So what do we do now?" asked Mistry.

Karan thought for a while "I think, like you said, he might make a move tomorrow. Meera, I think you should come back here tomorrow morning. Tell your office that you'll need to take a day or two off. And Mistry, I'd like you to be here too, just in case. We can wait for him to approach us and then try and stop him"

The three of them discussed one plan after the other before discarding them all. Finally they decided that they would wait till the next day before deciding on a course of action.

The friends walked along the beach till the sun had set. They could see the loom of a star in the sky.

"Guess I got to get back home," said Mistry "Are you going to leave Meera at her hostel, Karan?" he asked

Karan and Meera were holding hands again.

"Yes," Karan replied. The young couple looked at each other and smiled. "After we have dinner."

"Well, I'll leave you two lovebirds to it then. Bye, Meera, see you tomorrow"

Meera waved goodbye. Mistry set off across the beach heading for the road. He did not look back.

Karan and Meera kept walking along the beach. The wind had died down a bit and the fiery orb of the sun was just above the sea. They stopped to watch the sunset, still holding hands. It sank slowly below the water and the light in the sky faded. Now the stars were visible. Meera pointed at the brightest one.

"Maybe Stella is up there, on that star," she said "looking down at us."

"If she is, I hope she is watching out for us," said Karan.

"She is," said Meera. "I feel it in my bones."

They left the beach and headed for a restaurant that they had decided on, close by the beach. It was a little early for dinner but Karan didn't want to hang around too late with Mansoor lurking somewhere around.

Chapter Twenty Four

Mansoor emerged from the shadows near the tide line, where the waves were pounding the beach. The wind was picking up again. He watched the couple walk away, hand in hand and his rage and his frustration boiled within him. Soon, he told himself, soon.

Mansoor had been hiding in the copse of trees along the beach. He was clean shaven, wearing a new set of clothes and he had trimmed his hair. The overcoat and grenades he had hidden in a little hole he had dug under one of the trees. When Karan and his two friends had walked on to the beach, he had spotted them quickly. He had been expecting them. Although he had made no definite plan, he knew that after he had stalked Mistry that they would come looking for him. Mansoor had also guessed that Meera would immediately call Karan and tell him about his phone call. What he had not anticipated was that she would come along with Mistry and Karan to search for him. He was totally unaware that police and army personnel had been following Meera, thanks to Joseph, the romantic waiter.

The plain clothes police man assigned to follow Meera had overheard the conversation and had passed on the information to his two army colleagues who were also present on the beach. They agreed with the three friends that Mansoor was somewhere nearby. The army was also keen to get him back and had assigned their own men to work with the police.

Unfortunately the plain clothes man did not over hear Meera's deduction about Mansoor's disguise. Or else he and his colleagues from the army might have noticed the tall, clean shaven and well dressed young man now walking slowly down the beach.

Mansoor walked up to the road and looked around him. There was no sign of Karan and Meera but he did not expect to see them. He was making his plans for tomorrow. Today he was going to find some food to eat and using, the last of his money which had been in his pockets since the time he had escaped from the army court. He was going to buy himself a bottle of whiskey and drink it on the beach. Lately, he had been having some strange dreams. He hoped the whiskey would help him find oblivion tonight. Tomorrow night it wouldn't matter.

Mansoor had used up most of his money in buying a fresh set of clothes and some shaving equipment. He had also bought some fruits and snacks for himself. Now his money was almost over but he had a feeling he wouldn't need it after tomorrow.

Mansoor went into a cheap restaurant and ordered a chicken dish and a loaf of bread. He noticed the way the waiter was looking at him and the ex-soldier was amused. He was much too well dressed for this class of restaurant. When the food came, Mansoor ate hungrily, dipping the soft bread into the curry and chewing slowly. His mouth filled with juices and he swallowed and ate again and again. When he was done, he paid the bill and left a modest tip for the waiter. He strolled along the pavement, feeling pleasantly full, yet another kind of hunger was gnawing at him.

At the liquor store he stood in line and again he noticed the looks that the people around him gave him. Well to do people did not stand in line to buy liquor, they got someone else to do it for them. In front of him a rough looking character made pointed, insulting remarks about Mansoor and his friends burst out laughing. Mansoor ignored them. He knew that he had the power to make them stop laughing for ever simply by pulling out the gun tucked in his waistband and using it on them. But he had other plans. Nothing was going to stop him from putting those plans into action.

Finally he reached the window and handed over his money and got his bottle of whiskey. The man behind the counter gave his a taunting look, as if he could guess how much Mansoor wanted the liquor and pitied him his addiction. Mentally, Mansoor pulled out his gun and blew him away too, sending him to join his laughing comrades in hell. In reality, Mansoor hugged the bottle of whiskey in its brown paper wrapping close to his chest, the musical sloshing of the liquid in the bottle music to his ears. He made his way away from the store and down the road to the beach, keeping the suspicious looking package from the eyes of passer bys. When he reached the beach he walked along the sand to his copse of trees. He kept walking past the trees and then turned and walked in the opposite direction, passing the trees once more and checking to see that no one was following or watching him. Then he turned around quickly again and headed into the copse of trees.

Finding the place where had had hidden his old clothes, Mansoor quickly changed into them, taking good care to fold his new clothes carefully before keeping them away. Then he sat down, his back against the broad trunk of the trees, feeling its gnarled bark bite against his skin. He opened his whiskey and took a swig of the fiery liquid, choking a little after he swallowed and coughing heavily. He put the bottle to his mouth again and swallowed to more mouthfuls before lowering it and then he wiped his chin with the back of his hand and belched. Already his mind was fogging and he knew that black oblivion would come. He peered through the trees again, looking for the star which had haunted him every night that he had spent on the beach. After a bit of searching he spotted it, nestled between the enveloping leaves of a tree.

Mansoor stared at the star, so bright and so tantalizingly mysterious. Sirius, the dog star. A fragment of rambling memory stirred in his head and he remembered his mother pointing the star out to him one dark night. They had been walking back home from the village market. He must have been six or seven years old and he had never been out this late before. The sun had already set and the shadows were lengthening. The dark silhouettes of the scarecrows in the fields had frightened him and he clung to his mother. She was tried and weary and to comfort the child, she had pointed to the bright star in the sky.

"See that star?" she told him "you can see that star anywhere in the world at night. It means someone is watching over you."

The child was intrigued and he stopped his fussing and looked at the bright blue diamond in the sky.

"Who?" he asked "Who is watching? God?"

"Someone," she said. "You don't have to worry."

Seeing that the child was about to cry again she added, "As long as you are good."

That stopped the child again and he began to think.

"Are you good?" asked his mother and they walked the remaining distance in silence, the boy holding tight to his mother's hand, his little legs moving quickly to match his mother's larger strides, his face turning every now and again to gaze at the watching star in fearful awe and wonder.

Now, many, many years later Mansoor gazed at the same star and wondered, had he been good? Not very, he thought. But he had saved lives and risked his own in the process. Surely that counted a lot? The star had moved in the sky and was lost in the trees. Mansoor got up, carrying his bottle of whiskey in his hand and walked out of the little group of trees onto the beach. The whisky bottle was now almost half empty. He raised it his lips and took another swallow and then walked to the water's edge.

The star was hanging over the immense ocean. Waves crashed into the beach, the surf glowing in the dark night. The wind had picked up and its keening whine merged with the thunder of the waves. Mansoor sat down on the sand. Little wavelets rode up the beach to lap at his feet. The silting sand moved all around him. He gazed at the star and the mysterious ocean, stretching into the distance to strange lands.

He thought about the lady from the star, the same one he had seen every night for three nights in a row. Or had he dreamt of her? He could not be sure. He drank from the bottle again. She had spoken to him, told him what she wanted him to do. He didn't want to listen but he didn't want her to go away either. Mansoor wondered if she would come again tonight. If he waited long enough, she would.

He drank steadily form the bottle, watching the star trace its slow arc across the heavens. When the bottle was empty he threw it into the waves who first brought it back to him and then swept it away. Slowly it filled with water and sank into the depths. Mansoor's eyes were growing heavy and his head ached. Gradually, involuntarily, his eyes began to close. He tried to jerk them open but his attempts grew weaker and soon his eyes were closed and he dozed, his head hanging down.

Suddenly Mansoor woke with a start. He was wide awake instantly and has his eyes focused he could see her standing in front of him. He got to his feet hurriedly. She was standing there, several feet above the waves. She was wrapped in robes and her hair hung loose across her shoulders. On each of her shoulders there was a star, twinkling, it blue light falling over her.

"Mansoor," she whispered her voice soft as a sea breeze. It caressed his cheek and slipped in to his ears and he shivered in delight.

"Mansoor," she whispered again and he moaned. He would do whatever she wanted, as long as she stayed with him, as long as he could hear her voice singing in his ear. He listened, his face suffused with passion, glowing from within, and she told him what she wanted him to do.

Chapter Twenty Five

The morning tide was low and sea birds hopped along the beach, pecking at the sand, at the little sea crabs scurrying along, desperately scrabbling to go from one mud hole to the next before they were swallowed up by the birds. One of the crabs bumped into something hard and resilient at the same time. It scurried up a leg and then went further, climbing up the body.

A squawking sea bird, walking daintily on its legs, squeaked its displeasure. Mansoor woke with start and jumped up, brushing at his clothes. He knocked the crab down and the bird, quick as lightning, reached out with its neck and gulped it down. Mansoor turned, looking wildly up and down the beach. His clothes were soaked and covered with sand. How had he come here? Quickly, he turned and walked to the trees at the end of the beach. It was dawn and there were a few people on the beach.

Mansoor reached the trees and threw himself down on the sand. He crawled on all fours to a tree trunk and sat up, leaning his back against the tree. He breathed heavily. His chest felt thick and heavy and he was struggling to breathe.

He closed his eyes and dozed again. When he opened his eyes again, it was an hour later. He staggered back on to the beach and made his way to the public toilets. He washed his face and cleaned the mud from his clothes and slowly he began to revive. He looked up the sky through the branches of the trees surrounding him. The sky was cloudy, thick, dark low hanging clouds, pregnant with rain. Good, he told himself. Tonight there would be no stars. Tonight it would be full dark. And tonight he would do what he had come for.

Chapter Twenty Six

Mistry leaned on the bell of Karan's apartment till his friend opened, the door, bleary eyed, dressed in shorts and T shirt.

It was barely seven in the morning. "What on earth are you doing here so early?" asked Karan.

"Are you alone?" asked Mistry peering over Karan's shoulder in to the apartment.

"Of course I'm alone," said Karan crossly.

"Good," said Mistry, brushing past his friend and walking in past the door. "Listen, we have a major problem. The directors of Peerless have been arrested on suspicions of bribery. It's share value dropped more than 25 percent yesterday. You've lost a lot of money already. What do you want to do?"

Karan stared at his friend, trying to take in what he was telling him. It sank in slowly.

"What do you think will happen?" he asked Mistry.

"Well, Peerless has issued a statement saying that it is innocent on any wrong doing. It will fight the indictment. But till it clears its name its shares are going to take a hammering."

"What do you advise?" Karan asked, shaken.

"Peerless has a lot of assets. They own undeveloped real estate but they're not going to be able to exploit it with their scandal hanging over them. No bank is going to lend them any money till they clear their name. And if they are found guilty, they will have to sell their assets to pay off their fines and the interest on their existing loans. But what do you foresee? You've got to go by your own instincts. That's how we've played the game so far."

Karan ran his hands through his hair.

"I don't foresee anything," he said. He tried to remember the prophetic tune that he had heard so often but it wouldn't come to him. With a growing sense of panic he realized that it had completely slipped from his mind. When had heard it last? He tried to think clearly and finally it came to him. When he had looked down from his window and seen Mansoor on the street, looking up at him. That was when he had heard the tune last. But what was the tune? With a sense of despair he realized that he just could not recall it. He shook his head in sorrow.

"What is it?" asked Mistry anxiously.

"I don't know," said Karan. He was silent for some time, fighting the turmoil within him. Then he got a grip on himself. It was only money after all.

"Mistry," Karan spoke calmly. "Sell all my shares in Peerless right now. When the price falls to a quarter of the original price, use all the money to buy back as many shares as you can."

Mistry's eyes almost popped out of his head. "Do you know what you are doing?" he asked, staring in amazement at Karan.

"No," Karan admitted. "I don't foresee anything, but I'm just going to go with my instinct."

"That's a lot of money you're playing with. You could lose everything," warned his friend.

Karan shrugged. "Do you believe that a person can change his destiny?" he asked

"No," said Mistry.

"Stella believed that it was possible"

"Focus, Karan, focus," said Mistry impatiently." What we are dealing with are real issues."

"I believe that a person shapes his own destiny. Karma, if you will."

Now it was Mistry's turn to shrug "Okay, if that's the way you want. I'll be back later and then we'll discuss our other problem"

"What other problem?" asked Karan, alarmed?

"Helloooo!" said Mistry "Mansoor remember? Last night we concluded that tonight is the night he's going to try and kill you"

"Oh yeah," said Karan

"How can you be so calm?"

Karan smiled, "Good karma. See you after breakfast"

Mistry went out the door shaking his head and muttering to himself.

Chapter Twenty Seven

Karan showered and changed his clothes and fried two eggs which he ate with toast. Meera said she would be here around ten and Mistry would be here at that time too. He wondered what they would do. The only thing that they had managed to agree on yesterday was that they had no plan. This morning they would sit and discuss the possibilities and decide what to do. One thing Meera did not want and had begged Karan not to do was to call the police. Although Mistry wanted him to do just that, Meera had pleaded that she wanted a chance to talk to Mansoor, make him give himself up rather than be arrested. Things might go easier for him. Karan was not sure but he was inclined to go with what Meera said. It seemed the right thing to.

After he had finished his meal, Karan went to the window and peered down at the road. There was no one he could see dressed in an overcoat. Meera was probably right; the overcoat was an effective disguise when it wasn't worn.

Karan walked over to his favorite armchair and sat heavily on it, reclining back, resting the palms of his hands over his head, He was still sitting that way when the doorbell rang. It was Meera and she was carrying a bag full of apples.

"You seem to feel the need to feed me," said Karan and she laughed, setting the bag down on the table.

They chatted for a while, not raising the topic of Mansoor. Karan had left the door of the flat open and after a while Mistry walked in, wearing fresh clothes and with the satisfied air of a man who has had a good meal in the very recent past. He caught sight of the apples lying on the table.

"Great," said the well fed stockbroker. "I hope there's plenty of ice cream left over. Apples go very well with ice cream."

"Sit down, Mistry" said Karan, "and let's talk seriously."

Misty took an apple and sat down. He took a large bite of the fruit and munched furiously. "I'm listening" he said, his mouth full.

"Okay," said Karan, "first of all, Mistry thanks a lot for being with us. I know that this is not your problem"

Mistry waved his hands in the air, "It's nothing," he mumbled his mouth full of fruit.

"We concluded that Mansoor would most likely make some kind of move tonight. There's a big storm coming and he can't stay on the beach much longer. I suggest that we spend the night on the beach. Try and force him to make a move"

"Are you saying we should sleep on the beach?" asked Meera, surprised

"No, there's a restaurant on the beach which is attached to a hotel. It's open all night. I thought we could hang around there and every now and again stroll on the beach. We expect Mansoor to be watching and he doesn't know that we are expecting him to show up tonight."

"At least we have a plan" said Mistry, putting the last bit of the apple back on the table. "What if he doesn't make an appearance tonight?"

Do we do the same thing again tomorrow and every night till he turns up?"

"If he doesn't turn up tonight, we go to the police tomorrow and tell them what we know," Karan said, looking at Meera.

"I agree," said Meera, nodding her head.

"So we don't really have much to do today," said Mistry. "I'll be off to the office and be back around five in the afternoon. Save some ice cream for me."

He got up and headed for the door. "You two have a good time" he said, winking at Karan.

The door closed and Karan and Meera were alone in the flat. There was an awkward silence and then Karan said,

"Let's go out. We'll spend the day at the mall and maybe watch a movie or something"

"Sure," said Meera, ducking her head to hide her smile at Karan's sudden awkwardness.

They spent the day wandering around the mall, window shopping. Karan bought Meera a CD of Pandit Hari Prasad Chaurasia.

"Great music," he told her. "You'll never get tired of listening to him"

In return, Meera bought Karan a pair of studio headphones. They were far more expensive than the CD and Karan protested saying that he couldn't accept but Meera insisted that he have it.

"You're helping me become a singer," she said. "The headphones are really for me. It will help you to monitor my singing while they are recording."

Karan had to admit that the headphones would be useful and he accepted her gift.

They had lunch together in the mall's food court and then they saw a Bollywood movie. Karan couldn't keep his mind on the movie but Meera seemed to enjoy the film.

After the movies, it was almost five in the evening.

"Time to be heading back" said Karan, checking his watch.

When they reached the apartment, it was a little after five. They went in and Meera got the ice cream out of the fridge. They sat eating ice cream when Misty walked in.

"Hah!" he exclaimed. "Just in time"

Meera served him a portion and Mistry grabbed another apple from the table and munched it in between spoonfuls of ice cream.

"I've sold your shares," he told Karan "and placed a buy order at a quarter of the original share price. That stock has fallen off a cliff," he said shaking his head. "I really hope that luck is on your side."

"I hope so too," said Karan, looking at Meera, who smiled back at him.

After they had finished, they decided it was time to head for the beach. Meera had brought a light sweater along as it would be windy but Karan and Mistry were not carrying any extra clothing. On the beach, the usual crowds were there. The storm was expected to hit the coat late in the night but that had not prevented the evening crowd form gathering there. There must be close to a thousand people here, though Karan. Some of them were frolicking in the water; others were sitting in the sand enjoying the breeze which was blowing strong now. There were several games of cricket going on, with shouts of "Run, run" and "Catch it" rising in the air.

Higher up the beach, away from the waterline, there was a game of volley ball going on and further on a group of young boys were playing football very enthusiastically, kicking up sand as they chased the ball.

Karan, Mistry and Meera walked along the water. Karan wondered if Mansoor was in the crowd, whether he had spotted them. He would surely not do anything with so many people around.

Several meters behind the friends, three army personnel were walking, their eyes flickering among the crowd. They were armed though their weapons were hidden and they were also carrying two way radios. The army had taken over the job of keeping an eye on Meera.

"Let's go and have a coffee" said Mistry. "It's going to be a long night" They made their way across the sand to a restaurant. Seating themselves at the open air table, they ordered coffee and sandwiches.

The sun was beginning to set and the wind was strong now. Meera put on her sweater. The sky was over cast with clouds.

They sat drinking numerous cups of coffee and eating sandwiches. The sun set and people began to leave the beach. The three friends watched the crowd thin out and they checked the time on their watches. When it was eight, Karan got up and stretched.

"Let's take a walk" he said. Meera got up too and Mistry followed. Mistry was looking a little nervous and Meera was anxious but Karan seemed serene.

They walked along the beach. The night was dark, not s single star shone. The wind was strong and had a slight chill now and Meera hugged herself.

Mistry spoke and his voice was anxious. "I am beginning to think this may not be a good idea, Karan," he said

"I could have told you that a long time ago," said Karan, "but this is the only way"

"Why do you say that?" asked Mistry

"Would you prefer to be sleeping in bed knowing that he might break in at any time into your house?" asked Karan. Suddenly he stopped and turned to Mistry.

"I'm sorry, buddy," he said. "This is not your problem. You're a married man with a family. You should go back and be with them. He's not got anything against with you."

"I'm not leaving you here alone," said Mistry stubbornly.

Karan patted him on the back. "You're a good friend, Mistry."

"I'm probably just a dumb friend," he muttered, "letting you even think of doing this."

"Don't worry, things will work out fine," said Karan but now his voice was serious and he peered into the darkness all around them.

The beach was not completely dark, there were a few lamp posts which put out a spot of light around them, making a pattern of alternate patches of lighted and darker areas. They walked along this path, stepping into the light and into the dark.

Mansoor watched the three advancing closer to him. He was well in the darker areas of the beach, lying on the sand. He was wearing his overcoat again and the three grenades he had taken from the army jeep were clipped on to them. Tucked into his pants were the two pistols. He had checked his weapons earlier and opened and cleaned the guns. This was the last time he would ever handle a gun, although he didn't know that yet.

Behind the three friends walked the army personnel, following them at a discreet distance and taking care to keep out of the light. Mansoor had spotted them a long time ago. He could tell a regulation army haircut anywhere and it hadn't taken long to figure out that the army men were following the three friends. He wondered who Meera had spoken to.

Karan walked slightly ahead of the other two, peering into the dark. Now he was also beginning to feel anxious. Not scared, exactly but he wanted the whole thing to be over with.

Mansoor took out one of the grenades and gauged the weight of it. His three prey were not far away now and he guessed that the army folk were a about thirty meters behind them. Standing up in the sand, he put his weight behind his shoulder and, pulling the pin of the grenade, he threw it high in the air, towards the water line. There were no people in that area. At least, he hoped not.

The grenade hit the sand, several feet from the waves lapping at the shore, tumbled over and exploded. Meera screamed and Karan ducked. He pulled Meera down onto the sand next to him. Mistry was already flat on the ground with his face half buried in the sand. They were almost half the way between two of the lampposts on the beach, in an area of partial darkness. After a few seconds, there was another explosion behind them and a giant spout of water rose in the air.

Karan got to his feet and pulled Meera up. He called out to Mistry, "Get away from the light."

Dragging Meera along, he moved quickly into the dark, away from the water.

The army men had rushed towards the sound but when the second grenade exploded, they hit the ground, their weapons drawn. One of them spoke into the radio, calling for back up. They had powerful torches but wisely didn't switch them on.

They guessed that Mansoor had to be between the water line and the road at the edge of the beach and they peered in that direction, hoping to get a glimpse of his silhouette against the street lights. The three friends they had been following had also disappeared into the darkness.

After throwing the second grenade, Mansoor had run along the sand crouching low. He passed the place where Karan, Meera and Mistry were lying in the sand. When he estimated that he was in line with the soldiers, Mansoor took out his last grenade and removing the firing pin, threw it far into the distance, well beyond where the soldiers were crouching. The soldiers turned at the third explosion well behind where they lay and began to move cautiously in that direction.

Mansoor moved to where the three were lying. Pulling his gun out of his waistband, he held out in front of him. The first person he came across was Mistry. Kneeling beside him, Mansoor dug the barrel of the gun into his waist. Mistry shrieked and Mansoor spoke tersely, "Get up and move to the trees, all three of you"

The fugitive was close enough to friends for them that they could see his silhouette framed against the background light from the road.

Meera called out "Mansoor" pleading but he snapped back. "Shut up and move" Meera kept quiet and clinging on to Karan hand, headed for the trees. Mistry stumbled after them and Mansoor followed at the rear.

They reached the cluster of trees. This was not far from the road for the streetlights to cast a dim glow over the area. It was sufficient for them to make out the shapes of each other but insufficient to see their faces or expressions. Mansoor shepherded them so that they stood in a line and he walked past them, turning around so that his back was to the road and he was facing the beach.

"Mansoor," pleaded Meera again

This time he listened.

"What have you got to say?" he asked

"Don't do this," she begged. "Give yourself up and it will be better for you"

"I don't think so," said Mansoor. "Why were you unfaithful to me?"

"We split up a long time ago, Mansoor" said Meera, her voice sad.

"But I never stopped loving you," said Mansoor and now his voice was plaintive. "You know that."

"No," said Meera, "you don't love me, you're in love with the idea of someone loving you and I'm not that person, Mansoor. I never was."

"You're talking nonsense," said Mansoor harshly.

He turned to Karan "What have you got to say for yourself?" he asked

"Just this," said Karan. "Look up!"

Mansoor involuntarily glanced up. All of them turned their faces to the sky. They saw a strange light hovering above their heads, shining like a star and approaching fast.

"What's that?" asked Mansoor fearfully, turning the gun towards the light.

And then she was there again, suspended in the air, glowing with a supernatural light. Mansoor dropped the gun and fell prostrate on the ground. Mistry dropped to his knees, his body trembling, hands clasped together.

Meera whispered "Stella!"

Karan gazed steadily at the woman, swathed in white robes, who was looking directly at him.

Stella turned to Meera. "Look after him," she said.

"I will," whispered Meera.

The apparition glanced at Mistry who kept his head bowed down, hands clasped in prayer and supplication. Then she turned to Mansoor who was groveling in the sand.

She held out her hands," Come with me" she said. Mansoor got up on his hands and knees and crawled towards her, moaning and crying.

Stella glanced at Karan again who held her gaze. She turned away and drifted slowly towards the water. Mansoor got up and began to stagger after her.

There was shouting and people running on the beach. Flashlight beams swathed through the dark, their light swinging from side to side, searching, seeking.

The lady moved towards the water, suffused in bright light. Now she was over the waves and began to move over the sea. The waves crashed into the beach below her feet. Mansoor followed her, walking into the water.

Karan, Mistry and Meera followed and stopped at the water's edge. They could see the light ahead of Mansoor, leading him on. The renegade soldier walked, deeper and deeper into the water, his eyes fixed on the floating light. Now the water was at his knees. Soon it was at his waist and then his neck. As the three friends watched, the waves broke over Mansoor's head and then the water swallowed him and they could see him no more.

Meera shivered and then turned to Karan and buried her face in his chest, sobbing loudly. Karan patted her shoulders still staring across the water. The light had reached the horizon now and was a distant speck, like a star. Mistry was still shivering.

Behind them they could hear the sound of running feet and they turned and saw the three army men, holding flashlights and guns in their hands.

"Where is he?" one of them shouted.

Karan pointed to the ocean.

"What was that light?" the other man asked

Karan shrugged "I don't know," he said.

The third soldier spoke into his radio and all of them stared out at the waves. But all they could see was the rolling water, rearing as it flung itself into the sand.

Chapter

Later, after talking to the soldiers, Karan, Mistry and Meera returned to Karan's flat.

Mistry was still shaken. "What was that we saw?" he asked.

"It may be better if we don't think too much about it, "said Karan, "because we're not going to find any answers. Let's just call it a group hallucination."

"Group hallucination?" Mistry laughed derisively.

"We all had Stella on our minds and we projected the object of our thoughts into the air," said Karan, trying and failing to sound confident.

"You really believe that?" asked Mistry.

"No," said Karan.

Mistry was silent for a while and then he spoke decisively, "Tomorrow I am going to donate one hundred thousand to the home for unmarried mothers."

Karan couldn't repress his smile.

Later, Mistry went back to his flat and Karan and Meera sat together on the sofa.

"What was that we saw, Meera?" asked Karan

"There was always something special about Stella," said Meera softly.

They both sat in silence thinking about the girl who had made herself a part of their lives.

"It is too late for you to go back to the hostel," said Karan finally. "You can sleep here. Use the bed and I'll sleep on the couch."

"Thanks, Karan," said Meera, kissing him on the cheek.

"For what?" he asked, surprised

"For everything," she said and went to change for bed,

Chapter Twenty Eight

The next morning Mistry came by on the way to the office. He still looked a little shaken but otherwise recovered from the night's ordeal. He was carrying the morning newspaper with him.

"Look," he said, pointing out an article to Karan who had only woken up when Mistry rang the doorbell. The news headline on an inside page read "Renegade army officer commits suicide."

Below that was the main article.

Karan read:

"Mansoor, the army office who was once the hero of the tsunami was reported to have committed suicide by walking into the sea. Last night, Army officer had closed in on the ex-officer at the local beach. But Mansoor used grenades to create a diversion. Nobody was injured. The fugitive took the opportunity to walk into the sea. His body has not as yet been found. The Army issued a statement that they regretted his death and will investigate once more the events that led Mansoor, once a promising officer, to become an outlaw."

"That's the end of that," said Mistry, accepting a cup of coffee from Meera who had woken up early.

"Thanks, Meera. Are you leaving today?"

"Yes" said Meera who was looking rested and cheerful. "I'm going back to work today but I'll be here on Saturday. Karan and I are going to record the songs that he wrote."

"Great," said Mistry. "And when are you two getting hitched?"

Karan looked at Meera who looked away in confusion.

"I haven't asked her yet," said Karan

"What are you waiting for?" screamed Mistry in mock anger.

"Oh, I get it. You're waiting for me to leave. Okay, buddy, I'm gone and you get on with it."

Mistry was out the door. There was a poignant silence. Meera turned away and busied herself with cups and saucers.

"I've made breakfast," she said, cheerily, her voice a little strained. "Do you want to eat now?"

"Meera," Karan spoke slowly, hesitantly. She turned to him, her eyes shining.

"Will you?" asked Karan, nervous as a schoolboy.

"Will I what?" she teased, but her heart was pounding with excitement.

"Will you marry me?" blurted out Karan.

"Yes" she said, "oh, yes!" and then she was in his arms and they hugged and kissed and held each other close.

Later, while they were eating breakfast, they discussed telling their parents. Karan would go with her to meet her folks and then they would travel to his father's town and inform them. Once the formalities were complete they would set a date, but it would be within the next month.

After they had finished eating, Meera kissed Karan and left for her hostel. She would change her clothes there and then go to work. They would meet again on Saturday when they recording would take place. Karan was still very keen on getting it done. Besides now he had to think about the future, now that he was going to get married.

When Karan was alone, he spent a while thinking about the events of the last few weeks, ever since he had met Stella. The earthquake had turned his life upside down, he thought. And the tsunami had brought a sea change. He marveled at how suddenly life could change.

Finally, putting an end to his dreaming he got up and went to the piano and reviewed the material that he had prepared for the recording tomorrow. He phoned the two music company executive he had called earlier. Both of them were old acquaintances of his and they promised that they would be there tomorrow to hear Meera sing.

While he was on the piano, he got a call from Mistry

"Peerless share priced have fallen below a quarter of the initial price," said the stockbroker. "I've bought them for you again. Now you own a whole lot of their shares but it looks like it's going to keep sliding. The outlook is not good for the company. The CEO might go to prison and there is a chance that the company will go bankrupt."

Karan listened to Mistry with a growing sense of gloom.

"There's not much I can do now, is there?" he asked.

"No," said Mistry. "If you sell now you'll have a massive loss. If you hold, you might lose everything but on the other hand if the company comes out of this you could get your money back. That's a slim chance, though."

Karan sighed. He should have just put the money in the bank. He had earned it too easily, he thought. "Okay, I'll hold the shares. Thanks, Mistry."

The rest of the day Karan spent thinking about the future. Once again he had no money and no job. He did not think he would be able to pick stocks again like he had before. The only chance he had was Meera's' voice and his songs. If that didn't work, he would have to go begging for a job again. It wouldn't be easy.

In the evening he called Meera and told her what had happened.

"Well, I still have my job," said Meera. "Let's hear what the recording company executives say tomorrow. I think your songs are really good Karan. You've never showed them to anyone before, that's why you don't realize how good they are. Let's see what happens tomorrow."

Karan felt extremely heartened by Meera's words and her faith in his abilities. He sat late into the night, working on new songs and tweaking the tunes he had written. Tomorrow would be an important day.

Chapter Twenty Nine

The next day, Meera was waiting for him at the gate of her hostel. When his rick stopped she got in and gave him a kiss on the cheek. Karan smiled at her and gave the driver the address of the studio. While they were making their way there, Karan told Meera that they would be two people from different music companies present to hear her sing. Meera looked a little apprehensive but Karan told her to relax and just concentrate on her singing.

They reached the studio and went in. Karan looked for the recording company people but they hadn't turned up yet. The owner of the studio was there as well as the sound engineer who would mix the album. Today they would only record Meera singing and the music would be overlaid later on. Meera was shown the recording chamber and instructed on how they would process. She was given some time to get familiar with the surroundings. Karan and the sound engineer and other studio personnel went to the mixing booth. When Meera was ready, she signaled Karan through the glass partition. Karan told the sound engineer and gave Meera the thumbs up sing. Meera took a deep breath and started singing.

They did several takes of each song and midway through the morning the two executives turned up. One of them stayed till they took a break for lunch and then he shook Karan's hand, told him to send him a copy of the disc and then left. Karan was a little disappointed. The other executive said he had some place to go to but would be back.

After a while they took a break. Karan and Meera ate lunch at a nearby restaurant. Meera was flushed and excited but Karan felt a little more sober. Even though the recording had gone well and Meera was singing brilliantly, the two executives were not as enthusiastic as he might have hoped. Still, it was going fairly well.

After the break for lunch they continued recording. When there just two songs left the second executive returned and he stayed till all the songs were completed. When it was all done, the music executive put on a pair of headphones and listened to bits of the disc. Meera was sipping a soft drink and waiting in the lounge. Karan waited nervously for the expert's verdict. Finally the man took off his headphones. He leaned across to switch the player off and then turned to Karan.

"Nice voice and nice material," he said

"Thanks," said Karan

"Is she your wife?" he asked

"Not yet, she will be soon."

The music man laughed. "They say love is blind but thank god it isn't deaf," he said.

Fuck you, thought Karan but he kept smiling.

"The only problem is that this kind of music caters to a slightly up market, older crowd," said Jaisingh, the executive, "but let me see what I can do. We'll probably release the album in a limited way and try and get the songs some air time through the radio stations. Depending on the response, we might consider producing more."

Karan felt a surge of relief. They were going to publish the music.

"Just remember, no one really knows what the public wants and no one knows how a new artist is going to do. She's great, the songs are good, but the record could be a flop. Do you know what I mean?"

"Yes," said Karan. He shook Jaisingh hand and then the executive left, taking a copy of the disc. Karan slipped the master copy into a little plastic pouch and another copy he prepared to mail to the second executive. Then he was ready to go.

"Come on," he said to Meera who was leafing through a magazine. "What happened?" she asked "What did he say?"

"They are going to make a limited release and see the response after that they will decide whether to give us a contract"

Meera was excited "That's good isn't it?"

"Yes," said Karan. "Now all we can do is wait. In the meantime, let's go out and have dinner to celebrate"

Chapter Thirty

The next day Meera and Karan travelled to Meera's parent's town, which was just two hours away by train. Meera had spoken to her parents over the phone and although they were not very happy with the news that she was bringing a strange boy to see him, they agreed to meet him.

On the journey, it was Karan's turn to be nervous. Meera told him that her dad could be a little stern but she could handle him. Her mother would be worried but she would come around.

When they reached the house, Meera's parents were waiting. Karan shook hands with Meera; father, who was a stout man with a full head of silver hair. The old man was circumspect but civil and he led Karan to the living room and bid him to sit. Meera's mother had many of the same featured that her daughter had and Karan immediately felt an affinity for her.

Meera sat next to Karan and the conversation was halting at first but later flowed freely. After a massive lunch cooked by Meera's mother, the old man became positively genial and began to chat about cricket with Mansoor. By the time it was time for the young couple to leave, the older pair was comfortable with Karan. Meera's father kissed her cheek and her mother hugged her. Karana shook the old man's hand again and then they were off. Karan breathed a sigh of relief and Meera pinched him on the shoulder. "It wasn't that bad was it?" she asked.

"No" said Karan, but when I told him that I didn't have a job I thought for a moment he was going to bring out his shotgun"

Meera laughed.

Karan spent the following week with nothing very much to do. He was anxious to know the fate of his songs. He called both the executives who had been there for the recording. The one who had left early told him not call again. The other, Jaisingh, told him that they had released a few limited quantities of the CDs to several music critics and based on the response, they would make a decision. Karan was disappointed but there was nothing much that he could do. He spent the day in the felt not doing very much. Every evening he would meet Meera and they would have dinner together. On the weekend they planned to visit Karan's parents.

Saturday morning Karan and Meera took the early train to Karan's parent's village. It was Meera's turn to be nervous but she was pleasantly surprised when she met Karan's parents. When she met his father, she could immediately see the boy in the man. She felt a surge of affection for the kindly old man. Karan's mother was warm and welcoming. Later, Meera suspected that Karan's parents were secretly relieved that their son was finally getting married. Karan was an only child, like Meera They had been worried about him. After a lot of conversation and a big meal during which Meera met assorted Aunts and Uncles and cousins. it was time to leave.. On the train ride back to the city, Karan and

Meera chose the date for their weeding, two weeks from now. That would give enough time for the two families to meet prior to the wedding. They did not plan a big affair, just a few close friends and family.

The next two weeks were both happy as well as depressing for Karan. He had not heard from Jaisingh. From the five hundred thousand rupees that Mistry had given him for the shares, he would pay for the wedding but he knew he would soon run out of money. There was nothing much he could do except believe in himself.

The wedding day came and Meera looked splendid in her red bridal sari. Her face shone with a glow that no amount of make-up could have put there.

There was a happy crowd around the couple, mainly friends and family. a lot of girls form Meera's hostel had come, including Charmina Vaz. Joseph, the romantic waiter, gate crashed the event. He stayed to himself, eating cake and drinking wine, smiling happily to himself. He had even brought a camera along to take pictures to show his wife. Everyone thought he was from the other side of the family.

Mistry came with his wife and shed a few tears at the loss if his friend's bachelor status and freedom. But he was a different man now after the "vision" on the beach.

After the wedding, Meera moved in with Karan. Mistry's wife, who had become positively friendly with Karan now that he was respectably married, helped Meera set up the kitchen and make the arrangement to for their daily lives. Meera still kept her job and that was the only source of income for the two of them. Karan insisted on using what little remained of his money to pay the daily bills. He calculated that he had enough for the next four months after which he would have to rob a bank or get a job.

But the first two months of their married life passed in wedded bliss. One day, in their third month together, Meera took Karan to the temple. She covered her head with a shawl and closed her eyes and prayed. Karan took comfort in her serenity, not praying but understanding she was praying for him, for life, for love, for the both of them. He closed his eyes and thought about the last time he had prayed. He had asked God to look down on a poor songwriter down on his luck. He was still down, but God had sent him someone to love. This time Karan prayed for security and success and fulfillment. He realized that his last prayer had been in a church and this was one was in a temple. He didn't think God would mind.

When he finished his payer, he watched Meera. After a while she opened her eyes. Her prayers were done. She bowed deeply and then taking Karan's hand, she led him to the temple garden.

There was a group of children playing there, little toddlers and older children, some of whom were minding the toddlers. Their parents were probably at the temple. Meera turned to him and on his forehead she dabbed sandalwood paste. He bowed his as she made three lines on his brow. They walked on. As they passed the children, a little girl, slightly older than the rest saw them holding hands and giggled, pointing them out to her friends. The child ran and plucked a flower. She brought it to Meera. Meera smiled and thanked her, accepting the flower. She showed it to Karan and they admired it together. It had snow white petals and nestled inside, on a fragile stem were three little buds. Meera brought the flower to her nose and inhaled deeply and then she held it for Karan. The smell was sweet with a tang which invoked in him a memory of, he didn't know what to call it, hope? Succor? Promise? How could he smell any of that? But that's what he thought about when he smelt the flower.

They sat under a tree and Karan lay his head in her a lap and she ran her fingers through his hair and he fell into a doze and when he woke she was smiled, still watching him. They got up to leave the garden, holding hands, sharing the same dream.

Chapter Thirty One

The next day while Meera was at work, Karan checked his post box and among the bills and advertising flyers he found an envelope addressed to Meera. It had been redirected form her hostel. Karan examined the post mark and saw that it was from Gujarat. He wondered who could be writing to his wife. Probably an old hostel friend, he thought. He placed the envelope upright on the dining table so that Meera would see it when she came back.

When she returned, Meera saw the letter lying on the table. She exclaimed in surprise. "Who can it be?" she said glancing at the handwriting. "It's been forwarded by Charmina Vaz but I don't recognize the original writing."

"Open it" said Karan and his wife tore open the envelope and withdrew two sheets of coarse writing paper.

She glanced at it and exclaimed again. "It is from Mansoor's sister!"

Karan came over "What does she say?" he asked, intensely curious.

"I'll read it out," said Meera.

"Dear Sister" (she read) "a thousand blessing on you and your loved ones. May you prosper in this world and find God in the next. I am Naina, Mansoor's sister and

I write to tell you that he is back home with us and is well now.

He asked me to tell you this tale.

He was found floating in the water. A fishing boat returning from sea saw him and picked him up. At first they thought he was dead, but after throwing up a lot of water, he revived, but he had no memory of how he had come to be in the sea. He could not speak even, he had lost his voice. By signs and gestures he told the fisherman that he would like to stay on their boat and work with them. They were returning home at that time but they put him up and he slept in the house of one of the fishermen.

Next week when they were going out to sea, he went with them. They spent several days at sea and Mansoor worked hard. Slowly he regained the use of his voice but he still could not remember much. One day they met a fishing boat which was from Gujarat, a place near our village. He asked to be allowed to sail with them and return to his native state. They agreed, and he spent the next two months working on the fishing boat. Finally when it returned to Gujarat, he took his earnings and travelled by bus till he reached our home. We were so happy to see him as we had no news of him for a long time.

He tells us that he ran away from the army and he was not going to go back. Now he has been home for several weeks and works on a fishing boat. Every day he goes to sea and comes back in the evening. My parents plan to get him married soon. He is thinking of buying his own boat.

Mansoor bid me to write to you to tell you that he is well and thank you for I don't know what. He asked that you tell no one (except your husband) that he is back in Gujarat.

God's peace be with you. I remain, your respectful sister,

Naina"

Tears were flowing from Meera's eyes.

"He's alive." she sobbed. "Thank God. Somehow I knew that he was okay but it is great to get this news."

Karan was thoughtful, "I wonder if he got his memory back. He remembers you at least."

Meera wiped her eyes. "I hope he gets married and has children. He needs someone to love and someone who loves him."

"He'll be fine" said Karan, patting his wife on the shoulder. He felt glad and relieved.

Mansoor's apparent suicide had been a nagging ache at the back of his mind. The man had saved his life after all and Karan had no ill feelings towards him. Even when Meera told him that Mansoor was planning to kill him, he had never really felt threatened by the troubled soldier or wished him harm. Now Mansoor was safe at home and apparently recovered from his illness. This was good news.

The next day after Meera had left for work, Karan got a call from Mistry.

"Have you heard the news?" Mistry asked.

"What news?" asked Karan, thinking that his friend had somehow heard about Mansoor.

"Switch on your television onto a business channel," said the stockbroker

Karan switched on the TV and chose the business channel. On the screen heard the announcer talking about Peerless.

He caught the phrase, "Cleared of all charges" and at the bottom of the screen he could see the company's share price. It had shot up and was trading close to a thousand rupees a share.

Mistry spoke on the phone' "Did you see the stock price?"

"Yes," said Karan weakly.

"Don't even think of selling because this is just the beginning," said Mistry. "There's a rumor that Peerless is going to be taken over by a giant conglomerate so we can safely expect the price to more than double its current levels."

Karan was at a loss for word.

"I've bought some shares myself," continued Mistry, "and I'm positive that I'm going to make money on this. But you, my friend dare poised to make a killing. Congratulations!"

"Thanks, Mistry," said Karan. He did not know what else to say. "I'll talk to you later."

Karan sat on the chair in front of the TV. As he watched the screen, the share price kept rising. Finally, he could take it no longer. He got up and switched of the TV and just then the phone rang again. Karan picked it up and answered.

It was Mistry again

"You want to try and pick more stocks?" asked his friend. "Your prefect record has been restored, you know. Every single stock you pick has been a winner. Though with Peerless, I had to admit I had my doubts. But you came through, buddy. Let's pick some more."

"No, no, absolutely not." Karan shouted into the phone

"Hey, take it easy. It's okay. You don't have to do it if you don't want to," said his friend, startled.

"Sorry, Mistry," said Karan, calming down. "I'm done with doing that now. I don't really know anything about the share market and I'm not interested in learning."

"Okay, buddy," said Mistry. "No problem. I've earned a substantial amount of money through you and much thanks for that. See you later."

Mistry hung up and Karan put the phone down. Almost immediately it rang again and Karan answered, annoyed. He thought it was Mistry again but when he saw the number he realized it was Jaisingh.

"Hello," said Karan

"Congratulation, buddy," said the executive. "You've got the contract."

Karan almost leaped off his chair in excitement. "What?" he shouted

"Yup, its official" said Jaisingh. "I've just mailed the contract to you and it's a pretty good one. The test release was very successful so it looks like your music career had officially taken off as of now."

"Wow!" said Kara, "that is great news"

"I thought you'd be pleased. Now, Meera and you will have to sign the contract together and then both of you had better come to the office because there is plenty we need to talk about."

"Sure," said Karan "I've been waiting all my life for this."

"Wait no more." said Jaisingh. "Your future is here. I'll see you this week. Bye."

Karan leaped into the air, hands held high and let out a joyful yell. He couldn't wait to tell Meera.

Pacing up and down the apartment, Karan thought furiously. Should he call and tell Meera? No, this news was too big to tell her over the phone. Should he wait till she came back from work? No, he couldn't wait that long. He felt he would burst if her he didn't talk to her soon. The only thing left to do was to go to her office and tell her there. He could take her out for lunch, that was the excuse he would give for turning up at her work place.

He changed his shirt and comber his hair and was heading for the front door when the door bell rang. Who could that be? Karan wondered. He opened the door and found Meera standing there, holding a white envelope in her hand.

"Meera!" he exclaimed. "I was just going out to meet you. What happened? Why aren't you at the office?"

Meera walked past him and sat on the chair. "Why were you coming to meet me?" she asked.

Quickly he told her the news, about the recording company's contract and Peerless' stock value. Meera was happy but Karan began to feel that she was holding back a little.

"What happened?" he asked his wife again, "why are you home early?"

"I didn't go to the office today," said Meera, her voice serious. "I went to the doctor."

Karan's heart sank. "What's wrong?" he asked, anxiously

"Nothing's wrong," said Meera and then her face broke into the happiest smile Karan had yet seen.

"I'm pregnant" she sang out ecstatically.

Karan heard the oracle's sweet music in his head and then he was holding Meera in his hands and they hugged and kissed and cried and kissed some more and spent the day and most of their night celebrating their love and their happiness.

****

Eight months later. Karan is at the hospital. Meera has gone into labor and Karan is pacing the floor anxiously. He had been waiting a long while now. As he walked up and down, he heard, in his mind, for the very last time, the old, haunting tune. It grew louder and louder and he turned and faced the door of Meera's room, knowing it was happening. The music built up in his mind into a crescendo. His temples throbbed and he thought he would either have a stroke or be struck forever deaf and mute. Just when he thought he could bear it no longer, the music stopped and there was perfect silence.

The silence before a bud falls from a flower. And then he heard the most beautiful music in the world. For the very first time, he heard his daughter, Stella, cry.

****

This was how the meteorite was born, while the planets swirled in the cosmos and the stars shone. Somewhere, deep in the heart of the universe, a sun exploded in an incandescent flash of unseen light. A nearby planet, caught in a huge gravitational tidal wave broke up, sending large chunks of debris hurtling into space.

One of these chunks sped off into space in a direction that would take it directly across the earth's orbital path and on a collision course with the earth. A small pebble in the universe, a giant meteorite for mankind. The meteorite and its trajectory would be detected on earth. This time, hundreds of millions of lives could be lost. And more than a billion more changed forever.

Time to impact: four years, a hundred and seventy three days, seven hours and three minutes.

Can a person change his destiny? Perhaps destiny, life, is ever changing, ever shifting, like water flowing over uneven ground, always moving till it finds its own level. And then it is still and calm and placid. Till the next tsunami comes.

Destiny is in a state of flux.

Or is it?